William S. McCornick

Three Lectures on English Literature

William S. McCornick

Three Lectures on English Literature

ISBN/EAN: 9783337203184

Printed in Europe, USA, Canada, Australia, Japan

Cover: Foto ©Andreas Hilbeck / pixelio.de

More available books at **www.hansebooks.com**

THREE LECTURES

ON

ENGLISH LITERATURE

THREE LECTURES

ON

ENGLISH LITERATURE

BY

WILLIAM S. M'CORMICK, M.A.

LECTURER ON ENGLISH LANGUAGE AND LITERATURE
IN QUEEN MARGARET COLLEGE, GLASGOW

ALEXANDER GARDNER
Publisher to Her Majesty the Queen
PAISLEY; AND PATERNOSTER ROW, LONDON
1889

PREFACE

THE following Lectures formed part of a Series on " The English Poets of the Nineteenth Century," delivered to the students of the classes of English Language and Literature in Queen Margaret College and in Glasgow University during the Session 1887-88.

The first Lecture is mainly (pp. 29-53) an attempt to answer some of the arguments in an article by Professor Freeman in the *Contemporary Review* of October, 1887. It would not have been published had I seen since then any protest against the usurpation by Philology of the study of Literature in our Universities.

The Lectures on Wordsworth and Browning are not Essays. Addressed first to students whom it was my province to *introduce* to the study of these poets, they are still intended for a corresponding class of readers.

I have selected the poetry of Wordsworth and of Browning, as parallel illustrations of the operation of the Contemplative and the Penetrative Imagination of our century. The points of affinity in their contrasted genius are suggestive of the influence on art of modern reflection and analysis. These have given to both poets an apposite originality of method and subject.

The idealizing faculty of each is, as it were, turned in upon itself. The artist is not content to present his creation : he must at the same time analyze and

present the very act of creation. A
subtle consciousness has usurped the
place of instinct.

"The light that never was, on sea or land,"

had, though itself unseen, glorified the
vision of Chaucer, Spenser, and Milton.
In Wordsworth we find it for the first
time the subject of the poet's song. On
Lear and *Macbeth* we look, as we look
on Nature. In reading *The Ring and
the Book* we are brought into the labora-
tory, and are constrained to admire the
chemist's skill.

In the poetry of Wordsworth and of
Browning transcendentalism is frequently mingled with, rather than fused
in, the barest realism. Each poet seems
to take a self-conscious pride in his
power of drawing gold out of the
most refractory ore. Their creation of
fiction out of facts is in constant danger

of being artificial. It is difficult to recall the tact, directness, and spontaneity of the past. In style, as in conception, we find in both a remarkable inequality. Their inspiration is broken by level reaches of prose. In each poet we recognize the preacher; the philosopher—nay, the optimist—of his generation.

But the essential value as well as originality of both poets lie in the fact, that they have revealed 'worlds unrealized' in which we 'move about'— the one,

"Deep in the general heart of men,"

the other, hidden beneath

"This multifarious mass of words and deeds,"

CONTENTS.

English Literature and University
Education, ...   9

The Poetry of William Wordsworth,   65

The Poetry of Robert Browning,   .   125

*English Literature
and University Education.*

English Literature and University Education.

I HAVE often wondered, if I were to put the question to each member of my class, "Why do you come to study English literature?" and if it were frankly answered, what the answers would be.

I will pre-suppose in all, to begin with, an honest desire to know more of English literature; to understand and appreciate our English authors more fully and deeply; in short, to get culture for its own sake, for the sake of its influence in the growth of their intelligence and taste. But, while admitting this as their main reason, I think I may further assume, in many, a desire for results more immediately tangible and obvious than self-improvement; and perhaps the most tangible and obvious of these at the present day are,—the diploma which is gained by the passing of an examination, and the needful equipment for a place in cultivated society.

Both these aims are, in their place, legitimate. Examinations are a necessary test of our qualifications for certain posts or professions: the world, for public use at least, requires such a test. It is innocent and even laudable to desire a knowledge of English literature as a social ornament; still more, to use it as a means of social refinement and elevation. To raise conversation from the gutter of gossip and lead it brightly and naturally to such subjects as imply at least that we have brains and souls, is surely a worthy aim in the study of literature: an aim which women are specially fitted to achieve, and which, with such aid, they some day may achieve.

These two views of literature, then,

as a subject of examination and as a social ornament, are unimpeachable, provided that we do not surrender our first position.

Montesquieu has said: "The first motive which ought to impel us to study is the desire to augment the excellence of our nature and to render an intelligent being yet more intelligent."

Now, what I wish especially to point out to-day is the possibility of this primary motive, true culture, being overshadowed by either of the two secondary motives. And I wish also to consider the disastrous results of such a possibility —pedantry and dilettantism: results which neither "augment the excellence of our nature" nor "render an intelligent being yet more intelligent," but reduce both excellence and intelligence to a lower level than before.

We will look first at the danger of Dilettantism.

The excellence of English literature as a subject of study exposes it to abuse. Of all subjects it is the most generally interesting : it touches more nearly than most studies our nature as men· and women—our every day life and character. This is a reason, and a good reason, for its popularity ; but there is a corollary to it, which is also a reason and not so good a one. English literature, it is thought, is an "easy" subject. There is no necessity for an involved train of reasoning, or for prolonged application, or for a thorough grounding in its rudiments, as there is, say, in mathematics. It is generally understood to be a subject which can be taken at odd times and in small doses. In studying Algebra or Geometry, we cannot begin in the middle of a text-book and read a sentence or two here and a chapter or two there ; for we cannot understand a part without mastering all that has gone before. But in Literature, one can understand so much, can get so much benefit without this drudgery and difficulty, without any regular or consecutive training, and really without much intellectual strain to speak of. I need not illustrate this point at length, for we are all familiar with this tendency —to play at studying, to avoid the difficulties of a subject and choose those parts of it which seem easiest and most entertaining.

And if dilettantism is especially dangerous in such a subject as English literature, it is all the more dangerous in the special subject we are entering upon this session, the literature of our own century. Chaucer's *Nonnes Prestes Tale* and Spenser's *Epithalamium*, Hooker's *Ecclesiastical Polity* and Milton's *Comus*, are subjects which we naturally find some difficulty in leading up to at a dinner-table. Even Dryden's *Absalom and Achitophel*, or Pope's *Rape of the Lock*, or Goldsmith's *Bee*, is a little out of date. But Browning and Tennyson — even Shelley, Lamb, and Wordsworth—are topics which a moderate amount of tact may use to advantage.

Do not misunderstand me. I do not say that this reason has brought an addition to my class at Queen Margaret College this session; far less do I say, that, if it did, the reason would be quite so consciously realised or crudely stated. All that I wish to suggest is, that considering the tone of dillettantism which pervades our social atmosphere it would be strange if Queen Margaret College were alone untouched by it; and that the best way to escape it is not to flatter ourselves in our own security, but to realize our danger.

I would have hesitated to choose the literature of our own century for the subject of this session's course of lectures, had not many of you, perhaps the majority, attended already the courses on the literature of preceding centuries, and some, the tutorial class in philology and the history of our language. We cannot understand what is, without some understanding of what was. To take up the literature of our own time alone is, as it

were, to take up the third volume of a
novel. The story of literature, as of
history or of language, is one story ; if
we would read it intelligently, we must
begin at the beginning.

Our older literature has one pre-
eminent feature as a means of education,
in the difficulty we find in reading it.
We cannot read it by sentences. No
word may be taken for granted in a loose
way, as we treat our modern English.
All must pass a thorough scrutiny, demanding close attention and discrimination. The very differences of form,
meaning or idiom, reveal their full significance. It is in such minute study of
some classic work, say Chaucer's *Canter-
bury Tales*, where the words have all the
freshness of morning flowers with the
dew still on them, that we first begin to
discover what words really are, and what
reading really means. The study of the
history of words, and of the mean-
ings with which the masters of our
literature have charged them, is scholar-

ship ; and it is a study, perhaps equal to the study of those masters' thoughts, certainly inseparable from it in any University curriculum.

In disciplining our minds, in enlarging our sympathies, in educating our taste, and forming our judgment, our older literature is undoubtedly our better tutor. We go back to the past of Chaucer, Spenser, Shakspeare, Bacon, Milton, Johnson, not because it is better than the present, but because it is different from the present. The change does us good : we brace our minds in their times, much as we brace our bodies on foreign shores. The atmosphere of the past is larger and freer. There is about every present a narrowness, a provincialism, which can be corrected only by a knowledge of the past. One who has not lived out of his century is like one who has not lived out of his parish. Travel shows us other countries and other nations : in the study of a past literature we travel through time as well as lands.

The past gives us also a surer standard of taste and judgment. I do not say that the masters of our older literature are higher than those of our own time, but that the position of these masters is secure. The history of contemporary criticism is full of instances of its fallibility; it shows us how difficult a matter assaying is, and how often the most noted assayers of their age have taken gold for tinsel, and tinsel for gold. Time is the best of all critics: in the end, the only infallible critic. And it is among those works of art which have stood the test of time, that we can best refine our taste and form our judgment. The company of the living cannot but be mixed. The noble company of the dead is our only pure aristocracy. In their society we can best acquire a standard by which to estimate the living.

But to return to the danger of Dilettantism. No proof is needed, that its prevalence affords science a main point of attack on art at the present day. To say that our age is essentially a critical age, is but another way of putting it ; for more than half our criticism is nothing if it is not dilettantism. It has been part of my duty in preparation for this session's course to read many critical magazine articles of recent years, and I am glad to have this opportunity of revenging myself on their writers for the wasted hours I have spent over them. The vast majority might be characterised by the Scottish word " haverin' " — that is, writing with little to say, with no point or a point so minute as to be invisible to all but the writer, drawing distinctions and comparisons the importance of which is in inverse ratio to their subtlety, talking so long round and round about the subject that they rarely reach it at all. The good such articles in general do is, I think, more than balanced by the evil. First, they encourage us to read about literature, rather than to read it at first hand ; and secondly, they give us often a very false notion of literature, as a study much less widely instructive than it really is. Their terminology is so technical and remote from obvious meaning that, if we have independence enough, we often pause to think whether after all it is our dulness or their want of meaning that is to blame for the haze in which they leave us.

There is another evidence of dilettantism besides the darkening of counsel by jargon. It is a significant fact, which booksellers and librarians can attest, that a great writer's biography or his reminiscences is tenfold more popular than his writings ever were. Unfriendly critics of the study of literature call this, love of gossip. One of those used, the other day, the phrase "chatter about Shelley," which we admit to be a fair description of some of the disquisitions of which that poet is the subject; and the same critic adds : "A good deal of 'literary' talk now-a-days seems hardly to rise above personal gossip, sometimes personal scandal, about very modern personages indeed." [1] Now even personal gossip is not the worst form of dilettantism. It is at least human,—natural, not artificial as other forms of dillettantism usually are. It has "a certain veracity" under-lying it. It is not so important that we avoid it as that we avoid its becom-ing bad in tone, that is, avoid scandal. The word "gossip" has undergone changes which, like many in our voca-bulary, tell a tale. From meaning, first of all, a godfather or godmother, it came to mean an intimate or a friend; afterwards it was applied to light familiar talk between intimate friends or about in-timate friends. How it to-day comes to be usually applied to scandal, I will leave you to infer. But the point of this his-

---

[1] Professor Freeman in *Language and Literature,* Cont. Review, lii. 564.

tory is, that gossip was not essentially venomous; it was passing talk and anecdote about those whom we knew personally, whom we most probably loved and respected: a most natural outcome of our interest in them, discovering subtle traits and, it might be, faults, confirming or correcting our former judgments, which, sympathetically understood in the light of our friendship, might be misunderstood if heard by others. And so of literary gossip. Those personally familiar with a great author through his writings have a right to the anecdotes which bring the minor traits of his character in its excellence and defect more vividly before them, which help to complete and illustrate their former conceptions of his genius. Yet to show how such "literary" gossip may, far from revealing, altogether hide the author's true personality and greatness, we have but to mention the greatest British thinker of this century, Thomas Carlyle, whose name has been bandied about by those who have never thoroughly understood any page he has written, and who seem to be unaware that the subject of their "chatter" is a man whose shoe-strings they are not worthy to unloose.

One of the main causes to which we owe this unsystematic, superficial playing at studying lies at the door not so much of our universities as of our schools, and is the fault not so much of our school teachers as of our parents, especially our mothers. They, unless they are exceptions, and we are not now dealing with exceptions, do not expend very much thought on the subjects to which they set us. In most cases they follow the usual choice of other fathers and mothers; and in this way we all get a little English, a little history, a little geography, a little arithmetic (usually a very little—it is the one subject which requires some thinking), and then, as we grow older, a little French or German, a little playing, and a little singing. All these are good. It is important and beneficial in our education that we should know a little of as many things as possible; but it is admittedly as important and beneficial a part of our education that we should know more than a little about something. I do not insist that on some one subject our education should be so full as if we were preparing ourselves to profess it as a calling or business of life ; but it should at least be thorough enough for us to realize the full difficulties and full meaning of the subject—the height and breadth and depth of it as a whole. We should be so firmly based in its rudiments at least, that standing on that pedestal we can look out on a scope beyond our reach, 'and follow with our sympathy and appreciation, if not more closely with our understanding, those who have travelled further than we. And this intelligent sympathy once gained would not be confined to one study, but would extend to all.

This phase of education—"everything about something"—is not enough insisted on ; while the other—"something about everything" — has too much prominence. Our course of study is thus too much an *omnium gatherum*, a collection of odds and ends arranged on no rational system. Even good soup cannot be made in this hap-hazard way. Suppose our cooks to put in a little of this thing, and of that, and of that other thing, just in such quantities as came to hand, and for no reason at all, except that 'likely it will do no harm'! If we may ride this remote analogy one stage further, our educational soup is too often without 'stock.' It is, in short, a general sort of soup, no soup in particular. And the result is that our education leaves us—unless by some accident of fortune —with no individuality, with no special interest in, or hold on, life, because we have no special interest in any branch of life; prepared to see no deep significance in the world around us, as we have caught glimpse of none in our studies ; not necessarily dull, perhaps even clever, but characterless ; members of that large class of which Thackeray in *The New-comes* has drawn a fairly representative type in Miss Rosey Mackenzie.

So far of the danger of Dilettantism. Let us look for a moment at the danger of Pedantry.

'Education,' in its derivative sense, means a 'drawing out,' a 'development,' of our characteristic powers as men and women—our capacities of thought and feeling, our intelligence and taste. Examinations, then, as a test of education, must be a test of these powers, as exercised in the knowledge of the subject in question. Now, it is well known, that examinations, at least as usually conducted, are a better test of memory than of thought and judgment. If the mere passing of an examination paper is our only end and aim, or even our chief end and aim, it is not altogether illogical to reason as follows :—

"Why should we take the trouble of thinking and feeling for ourselves at all, why educate our intelligence and taste, when our thinking and feeling are done for us and we can procure intelligence and taste ready-made? Have we not got text-books and histories and Clarendon Press editions, where some diligent plodding and a good memory will serve our purpose, with the additional advantage that they do not vex our brains, if we have them ; and if we have not, who is the wiser ? Why take the highroad of education, of 'drawing out' our highest powers, when the shortcut of 'cramming in' the results of others' powers brings us to our goal ?" And if that goal be the mere passing of an examination, I cannot say why we should !

Those who uphold the present craze for examination and competition in our studies tell us that these stimulate our application and accuracy. This may be

true ; and yet neither may be of much
service in education, if our application be
misapplied and our accuracy relate to
unessential matters. Besides, examination
and competition stimulate those qualities
in students whose memory and pertinacity
are already sufficiently developed, while
they dissatisfy those whose intelligence
and taste lead them to seek in education
a higher aim. Competition—the in-
satiable ambition to surpass one's neighbour rather than oneself—is perhaps
the worst enemy true education has.
Its fruits are, in character vain-glory,
and in intellect pedantry.

But the dangers of examinations are
so trite a subject that we need do
no more than refer to them. It is
enough to indicate, in leaving dilettantism and pedantry, that each is what
Carlyle would have called 'a missing of
the point.'

It is not only that dilettantism and
pedantry do no good. They do positive
harm—and that, not only to our intellect,

but to our character.   Like other kinds
of idolatry,—that is, setting up dead
things and worshipping them as if they
were living things, putting the letter in
place of the spirit—they are forms of
deception; and intellectual deception is
closely allied to moral dishonesty.   Those
masquerades of true culture are in-
humane,—or inhuman, to use the older
form of the word when neither the
meaning nor the spelling was differen-
tiated.   The Humanities or Humanity
used to be the title applied to culture in Latin, when Latin was the
language of the literature of Europe,
before our nations had evolved each a
literary language of its own.   Now that
we have a literature and language of our
own, it would be well that the word were
kept if only to remind us that education
is not a substitute for our humanity, but
a development of it.   The seeds which
true culture fosters never grow to bloom
or fruit in the garden of either dilettante
or pedant, for love is not there to tend

them, nor modesty and sincerity to prune their branches.

So far of the dangers. Is it possible to avoid them? Can literature be made a fit subject of University education? Can its study be undertaken so as to become the training of our judgment, intelligence and taste?

Most of you are aware that at present the most vexed question in education—I should perhaps say, English University education — turns on the question whether English Literature is or is not to form, along with Classical Literature, a part of the University curriculum and a subject of examination for University degrees. Professor Freeman has written an article in last month's *Contemporary Review,*[1] in which he gives an emphatic answer to this question—in which he asserts that English Literature is not a subject for University training or examination, and gives his reasons

---

[1] *Cont. Review*, October, 1887.

for this assertion. As it was the reading of that article which first suggested to me the train of thought underlying my remarks to-day, allow me to say a word or two about it.

Professor Freeman's article specially relates to the appointment by himself and others, a year or so ago, not of a Professor of Literature, as one would have expected, but of a Professor of Semi-Saxon, to a Chair of English Language and Literature recently founded at Oxford; in spite of the fact, that there were already in the University one Professor of Comparative Philology, another of Sanscrit, and another of Anglo-Saxon. It is not, however, to the policy of this appointment that I wish to draw your attention, but rather to the lines of argument on which the writer bases his assertion that Language is a fit subject of University training, and that Literature is not.

His argument may be epitomised as follows :—

There is at present in the criticism
of English literature and in the affecting of it as a study, a shallow unsystematic dilettantism, the only outcome
of which is the expression of light and
capricious opinions regarding one author
as against another. For this reason,
English literature is not a subject for
scholastic examination. It is essentially
a mere matter of individual taste, where
there are next to no facts to go upon ;
where, therefore, it is not 'possible to
say of two answers to a question that
one is right and the other is wrong.'
Philology, on the other hand, is all facts;
it is a science, and is therefore eminently
suitable for purposes of examination, for
'if the examined knows the facts of the
matter in hand, it ought not to make
the difference of a line either way
whether his mere taste, his mere opinion,
agrees with that of the Examiner or
not.'[1]   Our alternative lies between a

---

[1] *Cont. Review,* lii. 563.

systematic science and a loose dilettantism. We must choose, in short, between philology, the history and study of words, and mere aesthetical criticism in which one man's opinion is just as good as another's. Can there be any doubt, therefore, as to which is to be chosen ; that philology is the only interpretation we can give to literature, if it is to be a subject of University training and of examination for degrees ?

The wise learn more from the criticism of enemies than from the flattery of friends. We have had our attention directed to some dangers affecting our study of literature by Professor Freeman's criticism. But we may now be allowed to offer a word or two in its defence. You will have observed, our critic tells us that the perils to which we are exposed are not only possible but inevitable, and that English Literature can never be a worthy subject of University study.

Let us look at this position. And

first we may note, he boldly assumes that in matters of taste one man's opinion is as good as another's.

To support this view the critic takes an example, not from our older classical writers, the judgment on whom has been by a long consensus confirmed, but from a nineteenth century, almost contemporary writer, whose rank time has not yet definitely fixed. "For instance," he says,[1] "I delight in the writings of Lord Macaulay, prose and verse ; I believe it is now thought more 'literary' to call them 'pinchbeck' or some such uncivil name. But I claim no right to pluck the man who calls them 'pinchbeck,' and I deny that he has any right to pluck me. My taste leads me to prefer verse which I can scan and of which I can follow the sense ; it is, I know, more 'literary' to delight in verse of which the metre and the meaning are, to say the least, care-

---

[1] *Cont. Review*, lii. 563.

fully hidden," and so on. It does not seem to occur to Professor Freeman that there may be a higher and a lower, a true and a false standard of taste; that education is possible as well in taste as in facts; that perhaps even Professor Freeman's own taste might be 'educated'; and that if he had had the advantage in his University course of what he contemns as a 'literary' training, he might now be able to scan some verses he at present fails to scan, and to follow the sense of writing of which at present the meaning is, from him, carefully hidden.

His position is so anomalous that it is difficult to attack it seriously. The false axiom that one man's taste is as good as another's would be paralleled only by the statement that one man's knowledge of a scientific fact is as good as another's. If Professor Freeman had taken for his example an older classic such as Spenser or Shakspeare, his error would have been more obvious. Within certain very well defined limits we may each of course have a certain individual bias corresponding to his individual characteristics, such as one to simplicity, another to grandeur—one to grace, another to strength ; but this is not the point at issue. For we at the same time admit an authority, a consensus in which they separately or together tend to meet. His dogmatic assumption can be at once disproved by a *reductio ad absurdum;* for if there be not a lower and a higher standard of taste, where is the essential difference between a boor and a gentleman, between ugliness and grace, between the ideals of savagery and those of civilization ?

Is it not possible that the prevalence of dilettantism which Professor Freeman so severely criticises, with its attendant fallacy of an equality of tastes, is largely due to the very fact that he will not allow the admittance of English literature to the Universities— will not allow it the serious study and the definite authoritative place which are its due ?

In one page he says,[1] " One might perhaps think that 'literature' of all subjects might dispense with any kind of teaching, that in matters of pure taste each man might be his own tutor, his own professor"; and in another page he cavils at the loose individual criticism of our magazine articles.   It seems never to occur to him that the two things may be connected as cause and effect ; that the very men who write those articles are graduates of his University, where in 'literature' they have had to be 'their own tutors, their own professors' —for want of better ; that if science or history were there as neglected as English literature is, we should probably have the same sort of unsystematic unauthoritative articles on them ; and that in matters not only of taste but of

---

[1] *Cont. Review*, lii. 566.

fact, one man's opinion would be thought as good as another's.

Even if a study of 'literature' were merely a study of taste, of style, it were unfortunate it should be neglected. It is more ; but Professor Freeman does not think so. It is his argument that, if we do not accept the study of literature as a mere phase of philology, there is only one alternative, to make it a mere matter of taste : that there is nothing in literature but the study of words and the study of arranging words.

There is not a hint from first line to last, that our 'literature,' as understood by its advocates, contains such a thing as thought ; far less, that the development of our literature is but another name for the development of its noblest and purest forms, as expressed through the greatest and the wisest of our thinkers. Is Shakspeare a mere phrase-maker, and Bacon a monger of words? Is Wordsworth but a stylist, and *Sartor Resartus* an example of German-English?

To this Professor Freeman would doubtless answer that 'literature' is but the
form, and that its matter belongs to the
sciences of history and philosophy. But
happily such a dissection is not in the
power of any scientist. History and
philosophy must be included in any
worthy study of literature, the matter of
which is as inseparable from its form
as the thought in painting is from line
and colour. It is this crowning integrity
of literature which gives to art the
immortality that science lacks, which
justifies Wordsworth's description of it
as "the breath and finer spirit of all
knowledge, the impassioned expression
which is in the countenance of all
science."[1]

Professor Freeman's position is more
unfair[2] than specious. "Beowulf and
Cædmon are, it seems, not 'literature.'

---

[1] Preface to *Lyrical Ballads.*

[2] I mean unfair to any sensible advocate of English
Literature as a subject of University study.

Milton's *Paradise Lost* is confessedly 'literature'; to study it is a 'literary' business. It would seem to be ruled that, if we bring in any˙ reference to Cædmon, the whole business ceases to be 'literary'; it becomes the forbidden study of 'language.'" This may be the opinion of Professor Freeman's 'man of straw': it is not the opinion of any professor of literature with whom I am acquainted. They would assert as confidently as he, that[1] a thorough comparison of certain poems of Cædmon and Milton, and of their relations to one another, would be a 'literary' study of a high kind; they would with him include Virgil also in the comparison, perhaps even Avitus, and they would

---

[1] *Cont. Review*, lii. 561. "For the matter of certain poems of Avitus, of Cædmon, and of Milton, has much in common. A thorough comparison of the three, and of their relations to one another, would be, one might think, a 'literary' study of the highest kind."

assuredly add to his list the Bible and Dante.

Again, " The only things that may not be coupled with ' literature ' are, strangely as it seems to some of us, the historical study of the language in which the books taken in hand are written, the comparative study of the languages which are akin to it, and the study of the earliest specimens of the literature of the language itself."[1] This position will seem as strange to the true student of literature as it does to Professor Freeman.   And even if this be the view taken by one or two irresponsible *littérateurs*, is the statement to the purpose ?   For is not the position which Professor Freeman really advocates somewhat like this ?—The only things that may be understood as ' literature ' are ' the historical study of the language in which the books taken in hand are written, the comparative

---

[1] *Cont. Review*, lii. 560-561.

study of the languages which are akin to it, and the study of the earliest specimens of the literature of the language itself.'

Professor Freeman sprinkles his argument with irrelevant truisms which any advocate of Literature as a University study will freely endorse. That the study of Language should be conjoined with that of Literature,[1] and that a survey of Classical and Mediæval, might profitably serve as an introduction to Modern Literature in a University course, I have never heard professors of Literature dispute. Something may even be said for the assertion as regards French, " that it is the business of an

---

[1] It is worth remarking that, while the full understanding of our great, especially of our early, authors involves a more or less minute appreciation of their language, familiarity with the science of words by no means implies the power to use them artistically. The style of the majority of our philologists is, even when technically grammatical, enough to establish this fact.

C

University to teach men the scholarly knowledge of languages, that it is not its business to teach men their practical mastery,"[1] were not this and other passages made to imply that the 'practical mastery' of his own language should be held of no account in a student's University standing.   It has never been found inadvisable in the studies of Latin and Greek to teach the writing of Latin and Greek prose.[2]

In speaking of the dangers of dilettantism and pedantry, I have already endorsed much of the criticism which Professor Freeman directs in his article against the study of Literature.   Where we differ is

---

[1] *Cont. Review*, lii. 553.

[2] *Cont. Review*, lii. 562. "Now I believe that I am right in saying that all the subjects of examination now in use in Oxford, from any survivals that may still abide of the old *Literæ Humaniores* to the last and most 'specialised' thing in natural science, agree in this, that all deal with facts, that in all it is possible to say of two answers to a question that one is right and the other is wrong. As long as this can be done, the subject is a possible one for examination."

in our conclusions. To him the teaching of English literature in Universities seems impossible for three reasons: that it cannot be taught, that it cannot be examined upon, and that it cannot be 'crammed.'

" All things cannot be taught; facts may be taught ; but surely the delicacies and elegances of literature cannot be driven into any man: he must learn to appreciate them for himself."[1]   True : they cannot be 'driven into' any one ; and if driving things into students is the definition of 'teaching' in our Universities, his conclusion is irrefutable.   Had he used the word 'educate,' or 'teach,' the premiss would have been fair, and the conclusion refuted.   It is evident that no student can appreciate a criticism of poetry or a principle of literary art by simply repeating it.   It is the *raison d'être* of any great work of art that it is the expression of something that cannot be

---

[1] *Cont. Review*, lii. 566.

translated, far less, 'driven into' any man. But the aim of University education is not to foster a state of passive receptivity, nor are its main appeals to mere memory—the supreme mental power of ' dry-as-dusts.'

It is a truism that the teacher " cannot hammer into a man so much as an ear for metre and rhythm; still less can he hammer into him the thousand minute gifts, the endless powers of appreciation, which go to make the literary student in any sense worthy of the name."[1] Yet, impossible as it is to give any one an ear for harmony, it is possible to educate an ear for harmony when it exists. The teacher can at least examine and illustrate for the student the principles of harmony, and, by sounding for him chords that are admittedly harmonious, aid and guide the development of his natural gift. In short, education—and I trust to speak for education in history as

---

[1] *Cont. Review*, lii. 566.

well as literature—is not a matter either
of "driving in" or of "hammering in." It
is a much slower and subtler task, and
demands more co-operation on the part of
the student, more activity of various intellectual powers. It is obvious that the
student "must learn to appreciate the
delicacies and elegances of literature
for himself" as well as more essential
qualities which Professor Freeman
naturally ignores ; but it is not less
obvious, if education is more than a
name in our Universities, that the
teacher must also guide and train him
in 'learning to appreciate them for himself.'

It is no argument against education in
"literature," that the professor of Literature often fails. His function is that
of the critic and instructor, to educate
what powers he finds in the student ; not
that of the Creator, to give him powers.
And as a professor of History may
occasionally meet with a student whose
memory is paralysed, a professor of

Literature may find a student's intelligence and taste so long deadened by mutilation, neglect, or bad example, as to be hopelessly barren for culture.

I am confident that literature can be made in our Universities a subject, not only of Education but of Examination. I maintain that no competent teacher or examiner ever has much difficulty, even in that department of the study which Professor Freeman superciliously contemns, æsthetical criticism, in detecting in essays and in written and oral examination the dictated from the original, the false from the true. An examiner in any subject so examines a student as to test, not only his mnemonical attainments, but his qualities of thought and power in dealing with it.

The assertion that in 'literature' the temptation to examine unfairly[1] is greater than in history or in philosophy is courageously absurd ; but it is explained

---

[1] *Cont. Review*, lii. 563.

by the narrow definition and shallow
conception of literature as " mere writing,
mere style, mere fancy, altogether cut
off from the facts of language." ¹ From
this contracted view alone we can
appreciate the analogy which follows.
" An examination," Mr. Freeman says,
" in contemporary politics, in which the
Home Ruler should be set to examine
the Unionist and the Unionist the
Home Ruler, would be an easy business
by the side of it : " ² an analogy which
seems more fitted to an examination in
history. Surely there may be differences of opinion between examiner and
examined without prejudice to either. ³

---

¹ *Cont. Review*, lii. 564.

² *Cont. Review*, lii. 563.

³ Professor Freeman admits this. *Cont. Review*, lii.
563. "Moreover the study of facts, the examination in
facts, does not shut out differences of opinion. That
is, two scholars may, from the same facts, make different inferences, without either having any right to
say that the other is wrong. And the knowledge of
such differences of opinion about the facts should be
part of the student's knowledge of the facts them-

We must suppose enough magnanimity in the examiner, whether in literature, history or philosophy, to give due value to a student's conclusions at variance with his own.

The 'facts' with which 'literature' deals are far broader and more extensive than can be grasped or imagined by one who resolutely ignores thought as its master element. What can this critic say of the development of the Drama, of the history of the Sonnet, of the origins of Chaucer's and Shakespeare's plots, or of the æsthetical theories of Plato, Aristotle, Quintilian, Lessing, Goethe, Hegel, Wordsworth, and Ruskin? The elements of greatness and defect in the works of Spenser or Burns are as much facts as those in the careers of Cromwell or Chatham. 'Mere opinion' has no wider

---

selves." Are we to conclude that Professor Freeman holds a theory of the equality of 'inferences' analogous to his theory of the equality of tastes, and that he would set the same value on the inference of a scholar as on the inference of an ignoramus?

range in dealing with the former than
with the latter, and at least as much
intellectual power is necessary to their
discrimination. The analysis of the
qualities of truth and imagination dis-
played in *Paradise Lost* is an education more cultivating in its influence
on the student than the analysis of the
facts which antiquarian ingenuity is content to discover in the *De Origine Mundi*
of Avitus.

Professor Freeman's last refuge is with
the 'crammer.' The study of literature
in our Universities does not suit the
'crammer.' He would spoil it as a true
study. One naturally asks : What true
study which he touches does he not spoil ?
Professor Freeman fails to recognise that
the 'crammer' will touch it only if he
finds it profitable for him to do so, and
that the examiner in literature has it in
his power, has it for his duty, to make it
unprofitable for him.[1] It is the pre-eminent

---

[1] *Cont. Review*, lii. 566, 567. "The art of

and prerogative excellence of 'literature' as a subject of proper education and proper examination, that its study is one in which the 'crammer' is useless, nay, in which 'cramming' is impossible. No one imagines "that there will be a rush of devoted students of English literature, disinterested admirers of great poets and great orators, with their whole works at their fingers' ends,"[1] either at Oxford University or at Queen Margaret College; but I am confident that it is as possibie to separate these students from the rest, and to give their powers and application of their powers their due recognition, as it is to discriminate between the real and

---

crammer has taken many wonderful forms already ; it will surely be its lowest—or highest—form of all, if to the endless forms of 'tips' on all matters, new and old, we add the last device of all in the shape of 'tips' on 'the Harriet problem.'" This apotheosis is only possible if the examiners by setting such questions make such 'tips' saleable.

[1] *Cont. Review*, lii., 566.

the perfunctory students of history or of philosophy. No worthy teaching is an easy matter; and one of the true teacher's hardest tasks is to keep at their due distance " mere mechanicals." The 'crammer' will attempt to invade the study of literature as he has " rushed in " upon other studies. But that we should therefore exclude the most widely educative, refining, and useful of all our studies from our Universities, is the counsel of despair. Professor Freeman gives that counsel with equanimity; it would almost seem, with satisfaction. We cannot find in it any source of satisfaction; we cannot with equanimity see our seats of learned culture become the mills of a learned pedantry; for we believe that when our Universities confess their inability to educate their students in subjects that cannot be 'crammed,' they will have failed to perform their proper function and will have forfeited their birth-right to the confidence of the nation.

I have occupied so much of your time in this discussion with a special purpose. For we are contending, not with an eccentrically dogmatic individual, but with a general tendency throughout education at the present time, pervading our Schools and School Boards as well as our Universities. The views which Professor Freeman assumes so confidently and expresses so explicitly in his article are the views which such men as Carlyle and Ruskin and Arnold have spent their lives in refuting—the views of those who would give us mere knowledge of facts instead of education, who would cover us with dry twigs instead of nourishing us as a living tree, who when we ask for bread give us a stone.

Knowledge of facts, nay, even knowledge of isolated scientific laws, is not an end : it is a worthy, an indispensable means. But, apart from our intelligence and sympathies, from our life and character, from our humanity, it is superficial,

skin-deep ; mechanical, not organic. It is
not what we know, or how much we know,
but how we know, how we have di-
gested and assimilated our knowledge
—not what facts we have accumulated,
but what they have taught us, what
powers they have developed in us—that
distinguishes an ennobling education
from a learned ignorance.

Utilitarianism is certainly not yet
the sole aim of University training.
It is not the function of an 'Arts'
course to fit men for special branches
of practical life.[1] Yet there is surely a
noble, as well as an ignoble utilitarianism.

The question of education—I mean,
of course, culture, apart from technical
or professional equipment—is as much
a question of character as of mere
intellect : true education is the organic

---

[1] "The University has nothing to do with the
diplomatic service or with any service ; it has, at the
stage marked by its Arts examination, nothing to do
with any profession or calling of any kind." *Cont.
Review*, lii. 559.

growth of the whole, not the mechanical exercise of a part. A common answer, I believe, among young ladies, when asked why they do not attend Queen Margaret College, is that they are 'not clever enough': the question is rather as to their tastes and sympathies. If these are in the right place, "brains will be provided." The difference between the cultured and the vulgar is not so much a difference in their quantity as in their quality. It is not in the amount, but in its direction, its attitude to such interests as our College offers,—in short, it is in character where the fault lies.

If there has been any unity of design in the remarks I have offered you to-day, it is to this conclusion they have been tending. See that the attitude to study be right,

> " And it must follow, as the night the day,
> Thou canst not then be false to any" *study*.

What that attitude is not, you will have gathered from what I have already said.

It is impossible for me now to do more than hint at what it is. In closing, I may indicate two qualities, characteristic of the true student of literature—a love of the subject, and a love of truth : on the one hand, reverence, on the other, open-mindedness.

" One grand, invaluable secret there is," says Carlyle,[1] "which includes all the rest, and, what is comfortable, lies clearly in every man's power: *To have an open loving heart, and what follows from the possession of such.* Truly, it has been said, emphatically in these days ought it to be repeated : A loving Heart is the beginning of all Knowledge. This it is that opens the whole mind, quickens every faculty of the intellect to do its fit work, that of knowing. . . . Hereby, indeed, is the whole man made a living mirror, wherein the wonders of this ever-wonderful Universe are in their true light

---

[1] *Miscellaneous Essays—Biography.*

represented, and reflected back on us. It has been said, 'the heart sees farther than the head:' but, indeed, without the seeing heart, there is no true seeing for the head so much as possible ; all is mere *over-sight*, hallucination and vain superficial phantasmagoria, which can permanently profit no one."

Wordsworth's assertion,

" We live by Admiration, Hope, and Love,"

applies to study as to the rest of life. If we rise from the reading of a great book with a due appreciation of its greatness, we have added to the chords of life and found one of the very best reasons for thinking it worth living : we have made a good beginning in our education, for system and application are obedient slaves of love. It has been said, 'It is the sign of a mediocre mind to praise moderately.' Those who always think the last book they have read the best book they have ever read, are often laughed at : their enthusiasm, if crude, is hopeful. It may show immaturity, want of judgment and balance ; but it is a far stage in advance of those who identify criticism with faultfinding, or fancy they have understood Shakspeare by turning him into an exercise on Elizabethan English.

And this attitude of reverence carries with it the reflex virtue of modesty, which distinguishes the true student from the dilettante and the pedant. The feeling of self-abasement may come upon us so forcibly as to be for the time enervating. One rises from catching a glimpse of the greatness of Milton or Wordsworth with a sense of mingled awe and shame. 'If such beings walk the earth, what the use of us worms crawling !' But this depression need not endure. Our natural buoyancy asserts itself ; and the memory of the mountain tops re-invigorates the inhabitants of the plains.

Open-mindednesss, the other characteristic we have chosen of the true attitude of study, is but a corollary of the former. The reason why so few understand a great author is not want of brains, but narrowness of sympathies.

The saddest sign of our times, the most hopeless of progress among those who are otherwise good and honest, is their frequent weariness or terror of thinking ; as if our intelligence were the one among all the talents God has given us, to be hid away in a napkin and never put to usury ; as if the love of truth were a prompting of the devil, and the noblest way to worship the great Intelligence were to worship our own prejudices.[1]

---

[1] "But so it is, the name of the light of nature is made hateful with men; the 'star of reason and learning,' and all other such like helps, beginneth no otherwise to be thought of than if it were an unlucky comet ; or as if God had so accursed it, that it should never shine or give light in things concerning our duty any way towards Him, but be esteemed as that star in the Revelation called Wormwood, which being fallen from heaven, maketh rivers and waters in which it falleth so bitter, that men tasting them die thereof." *Ecclesiastical Polity*, book iii., chap. 8.

We cannot do both; yet many try. How common a practice, to compromise matters by thinking with a side of our mind and never letting the one half know what the other is doing. Illustrations readily come to each of us of this dualism, this playing at blindman's buff inside our brains. Is not education, that is, true culture, but the solving of this dualism—being honest with ourselves, taking off the bandage and boldly using our eyes?

"There is a Wallachian legend," says Mr. Lowell,[1] "which, like most of the figments of popular fancy, has a moral in it. One Bakála, a good-for-nothing kind of fellow in his way, having had the luck to offer a sacrifice especially well pleasing to God, is taken up into heaven. He finds the Almighty sitting in something like the best room of a Wallachian peasant's cottage—there is always a profound pathos in the homeliness of the

---

[1] *Democracy, and other Essays*, p. 116.

popular imagination, forced, like the princess in the fairy tale, to weave its semblance of gold tissue out of straw. On being asked what reward he desires for the good service he has done, Bakála, who had always passionately longed to be the owner of a bagpipe, seeing a half worn-out one lying among some rubbish in a corner of the room, begs eagerly that it may be bestowed on him. The Lord, with a smile of pity at the meanness of his choice, grants him his boon, and Bakála goes back to earth delighted with his prize. With an infinite possibility within his reach, with the choice of wisdom, of power, of beauty at his tongue's end, he asked according to his kind, and his sordid wish is answered with a gift as sordid."

Britain has crowned the great names which form the subject of this session's course, has nominally crowned them as the source of wisdom, power, and beauty ; but in noisy, bustling, self-assertive times, it is hard to hear them above the screeching of bagpipes.

" There's not the smallest orb which thou behold'st
But in his motion like an angel sings,
Still quiring to the young-eyed cherubins ;
Such harmony is in immortal souls ;
But whilst this muddy vesture of decay
Doth grossly close it in, we cannot hear it."

I might apologise, for the warnings I have given you to-day, by saying that it is better we should criticise ourselves within our College, than that our enemies should criticise us from without. But I am sure no apology is needed, for I fear I have offended none. If there be anyone present who might profit by either of the cautions I have given, she will probably have passed it to her neighbour.

Wordsworth.

Wordsworth.

———◆———

Mendelssohn, being asked the meaning of one of his *Lieder ohne Worte,* played it, and said, "That is what I mean."

Whether conscious interpretations of art are more often useful than pernicious, it is important that we bear in mind their limitations. The duty of the expositor is to introduce us to the poet and then withdraw.

Poetry is emotion inspired: philosophy is a system. The poet has no more need of reasoning to plead for his verse than a friend of arguments to establish his character. In either case the truth is living. It cannot be explained. Its power is its proof. The interpreter can bring us to a point of view from which to look at it : the susceptibility must be our own.

Wordsworth has suffered more than most poets from a translation of his poetry into philosophy ; but the fault is largely Wordsworth's. His poetry all clusters round a few leading thoughts. The philosophic reader therefore sees in it the careful elaboration of a system, rather than the emotional expression of a great character.

Again, owing perhaps to this preponderance of thought, perhaps more to his solitariness and independence of criticism, Wordsworth was a conspicuously fallible judge of his own work. He continually wrote in verse what would have been better expressed in prose. There is much in his poems, especially in his longer poems, that is simply philosophy in more or less effective rhythm — thought which has not been fused in the alembic. This defect has the same root as the excellence which gives Wordsworth's poetry its individuality. The essential quality in Wordsworth's poetry is *reflection*. In his Preface of 1800,— which was a defence of his own poetry— an exposition of his theory of poetry, the poet describes this quality. Of his own poems he says: "Each of them has a worthy *purpose*. Not that I always began to write with a distinct purpose formally conceived, but habits of meditation have, I trust, so prompted and regulated my feelings, that my descriptions of such objects as strongly excite those feelings will be found to carry along with them a *purpose*. If this opinion be erroneous, I can have little right to the name of a Poet. For all good poetry is the spontaneous overflow of powerful feelings: and though this be true, Poems to which any value can be attached were never produced on any variety of subjects but by a man who, being possessed of more than usual organic sensibility, had also thought long and deeply."

It is Wordsworth's excellence that his best poetry is the spontaneous overflow of the powerful feelings of one who has thought long and deeply : it is the defect of many of his poems that this spontaneity of life is absent and the thought left cold.

With this *caveat*, let us first look at the thought underlying and modifying his inspiration. Reduced to didactic prose, his main *"purpose"* may be shortly summarised :—Between man and Nature there is, or should be, an intimate communion. Nature is man's heaven-sent surrounding, in whose silent influences he finds the truest development of emotion, thought, and character. We are born to love her. The child and mother-Earth are foreordained for each other ; but we become part of the world almost before we have inhaled our first unconscious breath of her generous power and joy. And what would have become in the reflection of after years the inspiring and guiding memory of our lives, becomes a void. The close artificiality of over-civilization breeds meanness, selfish cares, and transitory joys.

> "The world is too much with us ; late and soon,
>   Getting and spending, we lay waste our powers :
>   Little we see in Nature that is ours ;
>   We have given our hearts away, a sordid boon !
>   This Sea that bares her bosom to the moon ;
>   The winds that will be howling at all hours,
>   And are up-gathered now like sleeping flowers ;
>   For this, for everything, we are out of tune ;
>   It moves us not."

Nature is no mere inert accumulation of matter without meaning, but is the complement of man. Her infinite forms, her commonest phenomena of changing beauty or still grandeur speak not only to man's senses, but to his soul. The imagination, if duly fostered by a " wise passiveness," may read the " open secret " of earth, air, and sky. From the first indefinite and subtle influence, as that of a mother's lullaby, to the more explicit and reflective influence of after years, Nature is there to mould the character of man in a life of deep human sympathy and "vital joy."

With such a text, it is not strange that his singing robes should often hang too loosely round the poet, and reveal the preacher. It is still less strange that the interpreter should find in the poet who sings—

"On Man, on Nature, and on Human Life,"

the founder of a philosophy, or the prophet of a natural religion.

It will be seen how Wordsworth differs from previous poets of Nature. It is not that he excludes the views of those before him, but that he goes beyond them. Chaucer's joys of sense in nature—Shakspeare's analogies of fancy and imagination between human and outward nature—Thomson's deduction of the existence of a Divine intelligence from the laws and beauties of natural phenomena—Cowper's preference of a simple life :—these views are all contained in Wordsworth. But nc reaches further to a foundation and explanation of them all : he attains a creed compared to which these were but stumblings on the way to a conscious faith.[1]

One of Wordsworth's earliest poems illustrates the thought underlying his inspiration.

In the *Lines composed a few miles above Tintern Abbey*—included in the Lyrical Ballads of 1798—the poet first disclosed his essential originality. Published at the end of the volume which contained many of his worst failures, it was then little read and less understood.

---

[1] The poet's pantheism belongs especially to the period of his highest activity. In the *Ecclesiastical Sonnets* (1821) he becomes the verger of the Church of England. Wordsworth the man and Wordsworth the poet seem at times two beings. The one was in the habit of explaining away the inspirations of the other, as in the case of the great *Ode*. " It seemed," said one who heard him reading his own poems, "almost as if he was awed by the greatness of his own power."

Read carefully now in the light of
Wordsworth's after poetic work, we see
in it the epitome and prospectus of his
later poetry.

He is revisiting the banks of the Wye
after an absence of five years. The
poem opens with a description of the
sweet inland murmur of the river—the
steep and lofty cliffs which connect the
landscape with the quiet of the sky, the
plots of cottage-ground and orchard-
tufts which, clad in one green hue, lose
themselves among the woods and copses,
the hedge-rows and pastoral farms and
wreaths of smoke sent up in silence from
among the trees.

There is nothing bizarre or even picturesque in this quiet picture. Indeed,
in the best work of our poet of
nature we find little 'scene-painting'—
few descriptions of fine effects or subtle
skies.[2] He is not, as the professional

---

[2] In his later work, from *Memorials of a Tour on
the Continent* (1820) and *The River Duddon Sonnets*,

artist or tourist, on the look-out for 'views.' He lives with Nature ; he does not visit her. He takes Nature as she is in her retired and simple phases : he loves her for herself, not for her out-of-the-way graces. He is not fastidious. The 'picturesque tourist,' like the sensation-novel reader, has so little imagination, such feeble power of sensation of his own, that it must be stirred

---

we find a conscious lapse into description, coincident with his poetic decline. From Knight's *Life of Wordsworth*, Vol. III., p. 61, I take the following characteristic passage in a letter to Richard Sharp, written in April, 1822 :—" You recollect that Gray, in one of his letters, affirms that Description—he means of natural scenery and the operations of Nature —though an admirable ornament, ought *never* to be the subject of Poetry. How many exclusive dogmas have been laid down, which genius from age to age has triumphantly refuted ! and grossly should I be deceived if, speaking freely to you as an old friend, these local poems do not contain many proofs that Gray was as much in the wrong in this interdict, as any critical brother, who may have framed his canons without a spark of inspiration or poetry to guide him."

exceptionally to be awakened into life.
Wordsworth, with strong powers of
vitality within himself, requires but a
healthy sustenance.   In his poems, Nature is presented in her simple and essential forms.³

To return to our poem.   We come
immediately upon one of the main-
springs of Wordsworth's inspiration,—
memory, and the thoughts which
memory brings :

"These beauteous Forms,
Through a long absence, have not been to me

---

3 " 'And would he,' I asked, 'tell you as you
jogged along in the cart, which mountain he was
fondest of, or bid you look at the sunset ?'

'Ay, ay,' times he would say, 'Now isn't that
beautiful ?' and times he would hum on to himself.
But he wasn't a man as would give a judgment again'
ony mountain.   I've heard girt folks 'at come to the
Mount say, 'Now, Mr. Wudsworth, we want to see
finest mountain in t' country,' and he would say,
'Every mountain is finest.'   Ay, that's what he would
say."   Rev. H. D. Rawnsley's *Reminiscences of the
Westmoreland Peasantry.*

As is a landscape to a blind man's eye :
But oft, in lonely rooms, and 'mid the din
Of towns and cities, I have owed to them
In hours of weariness, sensations sweet,
Felt in the blood, and felt along the heart ;
And passing even into my purer mind,
With tranquil restoration." [1]

Not only does he trace the influence of the past in conscious memories. As our present character is the result of even our idlest actions, our present feeling is the unconscious development of sensations, themselves now lost to mind :

"feelings too
Of unremembered pleasure : such, perhaps,
As have no slight or trivial influence
On that best portion of a good man's life,
His little, nameless, unremembered, acts
Of kindness and of love." [2]

---

[1] It is unnecessary to remind even the casual reader of Wordsworth, that this note recurs throughout his poetry. As explicit examples, we may mention "*I wandered lonely as a Cloud*" and *The Solitary Reaper.*

[2] Compare the further elaboration of this idea in the *Ode on the Intimations of Immortality,* where the

And these memories of emotion under
the influence of nature's harmony may,
if used aright, so dilate all our after
thought and feeling, that we can at
times hear the harmony of a world in
which the worldling finds but discord
and ennui :

> " Nor less, I trust,
> To them I may have owed another gift,
> Of aspect more sublime ; that blessed mood,
> In which the burthen of the mystery,
> In which the heavy and the weary weight
> Of all this unintelligible world,
> Is lightened :—that serene and blessed mood,
> In which the affections gently lead us on,—
> Until, the breath of this corporeal frame
> And even the motion of our human blood
> Almost suspended, we are laid asleep
> In body, and become a living soul :
> While with an eye made quiet by the power
> Of harmony, and the deep power of joy,
> We see into the life of things."

---

poet accentuates the influence of the " unremembered
pleasures " of childhood on the character of our later
years.   And compare : " our thoughts are indeed
the representatives of all our past feelings." *Preface*
to *Lyrical Ballads.*

An answer follows to those who may think these experiences a mere hallucination. The joy and comfort they have given him are their own proof.

> " If this
> Be but a vain belief, yet, oh ! how oft—
> In darkness and amid the many shapes
> Of joyless daylight ; when the fretful stir
> Unprofitable, and the fever of the world,
> Have hung upon the beatings of my heart—
> How oft, in spirit, have I turned to thee,
> O sylvan Wye ! "

And now the poet breaks into a fresh train of thought, though intimately connected with the last. He recalls the past : his education under nature's influence ; " the coarser pleasures " of his boyish days and " their glad animal movements " ; then his youth when nature was to him

> " A feeling and a love,
> That had no need of a remoter charm,
> By thought supplied, or any interest
> Unborrowed from the eye."

These " raptures " all are gone ; yet he

neither mourns nor murmurs. Other
gifts have followed, "for such loss,
abundant recompense."

> " For I have learned
> To look on nature, not as in the hour
> Of thoughtless youth ; but hearing oftentimes
> The still, sad music of humanity,
> Nor harsh nor grating, though of ample power
> To chasten and subdue.   And I have felt
> A presence that disturbs me with the joy
> Of elevated thoughts : a sense sublime
> Of something far more deeply interfused,
> Whose dwelling is the light of setting suns,
> And the round ocean, and the living air,
> And the blue sky, and in the mind of man :
> A motion and a spirit, that impels
> All thinking things, all objects of all thought,
> And rolls through all things.   Therefore am I still
> A lover of the meadows and the woods,
> And mountains ; and of all that we behold
> From this green earth; of all the mighty world
> Of eye and ear,—both what they half create,
> And what perceive."

These lofty lines are the climax of this
poem.   They are perhaps the most explicit and complete expression in Wordsworth's verse of the central thought from

which his inspiration flowed ; that faith, called by some his 'natural religion,' by others his 'Christian pantheism,' which sees in the Universe not only the external work of God, but God himself —the divine spirit informing all and working slowly to a perfect end.

The conclusion of the poem is an address to his sister. There is, besides nature, another source of solace and joy,—humanity, especially the humanity of the domestic circle. This also is man's natural surrounding, the sphere of the activity and education of his vital powers.

> "Nor perchance,
> If I were not thus taught, should I the more
> Suffer my genial spirits to decay :
> For thou art with me here upon the banks
> Of this fair river ; Thou, my dearest Friend."

But it is in communion with nature that human love can best breathe ;

> "for she can so inform
> The mind that is within us, so impress

With quietness and beauty, and so feed
With lofty thoughts, that neither evil tongues,
Rash judgments, nor the sneers of selfish men,
Nor greetings where no kindness is, nor all
The dreary intercourse of daily life,
Shall e'er prevail against us, or disturb
Our cheerful faith, that all which we behold
Is full of blessings."

So,

"when thy mind
Shall be a mansion for all lovely forms,
Thy memory be as a dwelling-place
For all sweet sounds and harmonies; oh! then,
If solitude, or fear, or pain, or grief,
Should be thy portion, with what healing thoughts
Of tender joy wilt thou remember me,
And these my exhortations!"

There are perhaps too many 'exhortations' throughout this poem for it to be ranked among the most perfect examples of the author's genius; but I have chosen it for its 'exhortations.' My purpose is to show you the philosopher that you may be able to appreciate the poet for yourselves. If we have once firmly grasped the ideas in this

poem, we have the key to the rest.
We have here Wordsworth's point of
view ; and he had but one. His poetry
from first to last is the expression of
what we might almost call a stationary
personality. Among our English classics
Milton is likest him in this quality.
Shakespeare is of all farthest from him :
he does not look at life again and again
from the same standpoint : he rarely re-
peats himself. While Shakespeare submerges his individuality in his work,
Wordsworth submerges his work in his
individuality. Thus it is, that we may
delight in Falstaff and Beatrice without
understanding Jaques or Lear ; but
that if we comprehend any great poem
of Wordsworth, we comprehend all. Thus
also it is, that the one poet is popular,
while the other never will be popular ;
for all may find some level according to
their taste and ability in Shakespeare's
world, but only those who are prepared
to rise to Wordsworth's level appreciate

any of his poems,[1] and those will always
be the few.

There is evidence that Wordsworth
took more than usual pains in the con-
struction of the *Ode on Intimations of
Immortality from Recollections of Early
Childhood.* He was engaged in its composition for at least three years (1803-
1806); and its importance in the estima-
tion either of Wordsworth's poetry or of
his teaching can scarcely be overstated.
Like the early part of the *Prelude*, its

---

[1] Wordsworth said, in a conversation with Klop-
stock, "that it was the province of a great poet to
raise people up to his own level, not to descend to
theirs." *Satyrane's Letters*, III. In Knight's *Life*,
Vol. I., 176, we find Wordsworth's own notes of the
interview.

"It is not enough for me as a Poet, to delineate
merely such feelings as all men *do* sympathise with;
but it is also highly desirable to add to these others,
such as all men *may* sympathise with, and such as
there is reason to believe they would be better and
more moral beings if they did sympathise." From a
letter to Christopher North (1802). Knight's *Life*,
Vol I., p. 404.

subject is the memories of childhood and their influence in the moulding of our later years,—the close connection of the instincts and half-conscious delights of the morning of life . with the more mature and reflective imagination of its later day. Its argument is summed in the three lines originally prefixed to the *Ode :*

> " The Child is Father of the Man ;
> And I could wish my days to be
> Bound each to each by natural piety." ₁

The idea of the pre-existence of the soul before birth is of course Platonic ; but Wordsworth's use of it in this Ode differs from Plato's. While Plato thought of man gradually through life working to the ideal which he had left at birth, Wordsworth opens with the plaint that man's conventional life is a forgetting of it.

₁ The last lines of *My Heart leaps up,* a lyric which contains in embryo the idea which the *Ode* more impressively elaborates.

> " Shades of the prison-house begin to close
>   Upon the growing Boy ; "

until

> "At length the Man perceives it die away,
>   And fade into the light of common day."

The first eight stanzas however contain but half the argument of the poem. Were these all, the poem would bear no richer moral than Herrick's 'Gather ye rosebuds while ye may,' or than is to be derived from the despair of 'have beens.'[1] It is Wordsworth's 'purpose'

---

[1] Mr. Leslie Stephen (*Hours in a Library.* Third Series, p. 194,) aptly contrasts Byron's and Shelley's passionate lamentation over the departure of the "spirit of delight," with that of Wordsworth. Byron fails to recognise the higher uses to which the fading memories may be put.

> " There's not a joy the world can give like that it
>   takes away."

And, though Shelley still clings to the hope that his "dead thoughts" may be driven over the universe,

> " Like withered leaves to quicken a new birth,"

he yet bows before an inexorable fate that has cramped his energies :

> "A heavy weight of years has chained and bowed
>   One too like thee ; tameless and swift and proud."

to show that the instinctive joys of childhood may become more than a regret-
ful memory, that they need not be lost,
but may develope into something more
permanent in the imaginative reflection
of maturity :

> " Hence, in a season of calm weather
> Though inland far we be,
> Our souls have sight of that immortal sea
> Which brought us hither,
> Can in a moment travel thither,
> And see the Children sport upon the shore,
> And hear the mighty waters rolling evermore."

The two concluding stanzas of the
Ode carry on this thought of the con-
tinuity of childhood and age, and break
away from the region of regrets into a
pæan of hope and faith in life's later as
well as earlier years :

What though the radiance which was once so bright
Be now for ever taken from my sight,
    Though nothing can bring back the hour
Of splendours in the grass, of glory in the flower ;

Neither " can see any satisfactory solution, and therefore neither can reach a perfect harmony of thought
and feeling."

We will grieve not, rather find
Strength in what remains behind ;
In the primal sympathy
Which having been must ever be ;
In the soothing thoughts that spring
Out of human suffering ;
In the faith that looks through death,
In years that bring the philosophic mind."

Mr. Arnold makes the following criticism on this Ode :—

"Even the 'intimations' of the famous Ode, those corner-stones of the supposed philosophic system of Wordsworth, the idea of the high instincts and affections coming out in childhood, testifying of a divine home recently left, and fading away as our life proceeds, — this idea, of undeniable beauty as a play of fancy, has itself not the character of poetic truth of the best kind ; it has no real solidity. The instinct of delight in Nature and her beauty had no doubt extraordinary strength in Wordsworth himself as a child. But to say that universally this instinct is mighty in childhood, and tends to die away afterwards, is to say what is extremely doubtful. In many people, perhaps with the majority of educated persons, the love of nature is nearly imperceptible at ten years old, but strong and operative at thirty. In general we may say of these high instincts of early childhood, the base of the alleged systematic philosophy of Wordsworth, what Thucydides says of the early achievements of the Greek race :—' It is impossible to speak with certainty of what is so remote ; but from all that we can really investigate, I should say that they were no very great things.'"

Such a criticism betrays a misconception of the central idea of the Ode.

Wordsworth does not deny that "the love of Nature is nearly imperceptible at ten years old, and strong and operative at thirty," any more than that the love of a son for a mother is the same. Wordsworth's belief that the impressions of Nature during childhood are latent, for the most part not only unexpressed but unrealized, could be exhibited by many quotations from his verse.[1] Perceptibility implies reflection, and comes with

---

[1] The following may serve, from the well-known *Sonnet Composed upon the Beach near Calais:*

" Dear Child ! dear Girl ! that walkest with me here,
If thou appear'st untouched by solemn thought,
Thy nature is not therefore less divine :
Thou liest in Abraham's bosom all the year ;
And worshipp'st at the Temple's inner shrine,
God being with thee when we know it not."

This revelation of the unconscious sympathies

"That steal upon the meditative mind,
And grow with thought,"

constitutes Wordsworth's essential originality. It occurs *passim* in the early books of the *Prelude, e.g.,*

" By intercourse of touch
He held mute dialogues with his Mother's heart,
Whereby this infant sensibility,
Great birthright of our being, was in him
Augmented and sustained."

Or,

" He held unconscious intercourse with Beauty
Old as creation, drinking in a pure
Organic pleasure."

later years when the latent stores of childhood develop as a memory—

> "those first affections,
> Those shadowy recollections,
> Which, be they what they may,
> Are yet the fountain light of all our day."

As it is not Wordsworth's purpose in making us feel the joys "of all the mighty world of eye and ear" to distinguish between "what they half create and what perceive," so it is not here his purpose to separate *Dichtung* from *Wahrheit*. Our own idealised memories, not our nurses' or tutors' memories of facts, are his subject. "No very great things," these impressions of childhood, like "the early achievements[1] of the Greek race": all will admit this. Yet surely both, the germ and making of great things!

The two representative poems which I have chosen give us Wordsworth's

---

[1] The word "achievements" renders the analogy quite inappropriate.

F

point of view regarding Nature and Man. We see in them the strands of thought running through his poetry and teaching. To illustrate these by reference to *The Excursion* would take us beyond our limits. I must, therefore, be content to note how they express themselves in a few of the poems of the best period (1798-1808) of Wordsworth's activity.

We may range these poems in two classes : one, of Ballad and Narrative poetry in which the poet makes other characters and their portraiture or story the vehicle of his inspiration ; and the other, of Autobiographical, Lyrical and Reflective poems, and Sonnets, which are the more direct expression of his own thought and emotion. Yet this division is not more than one of form ; for Wordsworth's genius is essentially undramatic,[1] and his creations

---

[1] " In my treatment of the intellectual instincts, affections, and passions of mankind, I am nobly dis-

are little more than representations of his ideal or of himself in various circumstances of life. Matthew in *The Two April Mornings* and *The Fountain,* Leonard in *The Brothers,* the old Leech-Gatherer in *Resolution and Independence,* Lord Clifford in the *Song at the Feast of Brougham Castle* are as evidently the poet in a thin disguise, as the Wanderer or the Parson in *The Excursion*; and the Solitary seems to us to-day a Wordsworthian atheist.[1]

---

tinguished by having drawn out into notice the points in which they resemble each other, in preference to dwelling (as dramatic authors must do) upon those in which they differ. If my writings are to last, it will, I myself believe, be mainly owing to this characteristic. They will please for the single cause, 'That we have all of us one human heart.'" From a letter to Crabb Robinson (1835). Knight's *Life.* Vol. III., p. 250.

[1] Compare Wordsworth's opinion of Voltaire's work—

"Dull product of a scoffer's pen,"

with Cowper's picture in *Truth* of the aged cottager who

"Just knows, and knows no more, her Bible true--
A truth the brilliant Frenchman never knew."

Even in that exotic masterpiece of the poet's genius, *Laodameia,* Protesilaos preaches from the gospel according to Wordsworth ; while the noble *Character of the Happy Warrior* is as confessedly didactic as the *Ode to Duty.*

Perhaps the loveliest of his portraitures are those of another sex. Yet

---

Wordsworth's general indebtedness to Cowper has not been fully illustrated. Evidence of his intimate acquaintance with Cowper's poems is given in Knight's *Life.*

The following passage from Haydon's account of "an immortal dinner" which he gave in 1817 is worth insertion here. "Lamb's fun in the midst of Wordsworth's solemn intonations of oratory was like the sarcasm and wit of the fool in the intervals of Lear's passion. He made a speech, and voted me absent, and made them drink my health. 'Now,' said Lamb, 'you old lake poet, you rascally poet, why do you call Voltaire dull ?' We all defended Wordsworth, and affirmed there was a state of mind when Voltaire would be dull. 'Well,' said Lamb, 'here's Voltaire—the Messiah of the French nation, and a very proper one too.' . . . It was delightful to see the good humour of Wordsworth in giving in to all our frolics without affectation, and laughing as heartily as the best of us."

they also belong to Wordsworth's family, "through whom a kindred likeness prevails, as well of minds as of persons."[1] The value of these portraits lies, not as in Browning's in their insight into character, but in their imagination of a high and pure ideal.

Of these, the " Lucy " poems[2] are the first. Who the subject of them was, remains untold ; but that she was the heroine of some love episode in Wordsworth's life, can scarcely be doubted by any who have read the pathetic lines which close the shortest of them :

---

[1] "Vicar of Wakefield," chap. 1.

[2] Mr. Arnold has happily placed the five poems together in his *Selections :* a volume which includes little that the lover of poetry will reject, and excludes less that the lover of Wordsworth will miss. The latter may regret the absence of *To the Daisy* (second poem) and *The Kitten and Falling Leaves* as interesting exceptions to the poet's characteristic solemnity. Another example of his playful mood is the doggerel lines quoted by Professor Knight. *Life,* Vol. II., p. 273.

" She lived unknown, and few could know
 When Lucy ceased to be ;
But she is in her grave, and, oh,
 The difference to me ! "

I cannot refrain from quoting the longest of this group which Mr. Palgrave in his *Golden Treasury* has appropriated entitled : *The Education of Nature.* To those who are familiar with Ruskin's *Sesame and Lilies* it must be well known ; yet, as one of the most perfect examples of the simple and natural dignity of Wordsworth's ideal, it cannot be over-cherished.

" Three years she grew in sun and shower,
 Then Nature said, ' A lovelier flower
 On earth was never sown ;
This Child I to myself will take ;
 She shall be mine, and I will make
 A Lady of my own.

' Myself will to my darling be
 Both law and impulse : and with me
 The Girl, in rock and plain,
In earth and heaven, in glade and bower,
 Shall feel an overseeing power
 To kindle or restrain.

' She shall be sportive as the Fawn
　That wild with glee across the lawn,
　Or up the mountain springs ;
　And her's shall be the breathing balm,
　And her's the silence andthe calm
　Of mute insensate things.

' The floating Clouds their state shall lend
　To her ; for her the willow bend ;
　Nor shall she fail to see
　Even in the motions of the Storm
　Grace that shall mould the Maiden's form
　By silent sympathy.

' The Stars of midnight shall be dear
　To her ; and she shall lean her ear
　In many a secret place
　Where Rivulets dance their wayward round,
　And beauty born of murmuring sound
　Shall pass into her face.

' And vital feelings of delight
　Shall rear her form to stately height,
　Her virgin bosom swell ;
　Such thoughts to Lucy I will give
　While she and I together live
　Here in this happy Dell.' "

Those who are not thorough-going
' Wordsworthians ' will recognise, it
may be, too acutely, the serious defect

in even such a beautiful ideal as this—
the lack in it of that other side of our
nature, the social side ; a lack which is
the result of Wordsworth's character of
half-ascetic solitariness. Yet no one
who has once felt the thrilling charm of
these verses can recall them without a
feeling akin to 'exaltation'; without a
renewed feeling of repugnance to those
commoner ideals which err so far the
other way, for whom midnight has no
stars and rivulets dance in vain, where
sportive freedom has been exchanged
for conventional prudery, in whom there
is politeness without sympathy, pretti-
ness but no beauty, and elegance wanting
in dignity or grace.

We naturally connect this series of
poems with the lyric *She was a Phantom
of Delight*, in which the poet has drawn
from his own home the picture of the
child, the maiden, and the wife. First,

" A lovely Apparition, sent
To be a moment's ornament ;
.   .   .   .

> A dancing Shape, an Image gay.
> To haunt, to startle, and waylay."

> " I saw her upon nearer view,
> A Spirit, yet a Woman too !
> Her household motions light and free,
> And steps of virgin liberty ;
> A countenance in which did meet
> Sweet records, promises as sweet ;
> A Creature not too bright or good
> For human nature's daily food ;
> For transient sorrows, simple wiles,
> Praise, blame, love, kisses, tears and smiles."

And then, at last,

> " A perfect Woman, nobly planned,
> To warn, to comfort, and command ;
> And yet a Spirit still, and bright
> With something of an angel light."

It is this homeliness of ideal—this constant insistence on the fulfilment of the natural primary duties and affections within the reach of all, as the only source of man's true joy and dignity—which is the basis of Wordsworth's moral teaching. In his Sonnet,[1] he calls on Milton to raise England from her selfish-

---

[1] *Sonnet IX.* London, 1802.

ness and restore her "manners, virtue, freedom, power," because he travelled "on life's common way in cheerful godliness, and yet his heart the lowliest duties on herself did lay." As in outward nature, so in human nature, it is her simple and common excellences which are the favourite food of Wordsworth's inspiration. This homeliness of ideal—or more correctly, the qualities of character which were the source of this homeliness of ideal—led Wordsworth into theories of poetry which we may best understand by considering the criticisms which have been made against them.

I do not mean to enter now on a consideration of Wordsworth's much discussed dictum "that there neither is, nor can be, any *essential* difference between the language of prose and metrical composition." [1] If by ' language '

---

[1] *Preface to the Second Edition of "Lyrical Ballads"* (1800). The word "essential" eliminates such exceptions as the occasional use of archaisms, etc.

Wordsworth means 'words,' it is to-day a truism;[1] if he means 'the use of words' it is entirely false, as he himself shows in a later Preface.[2] It is not

---

[1] To Coleridge this interpretation seemed too axio-matic for argument (*Biographia Literaria, passim*); yet Wordsworth in his Preface does not explicitly commit himself to the other. The assertion was, in any case, an inadequate defence of his ballad poetry, and a rather involved method of attacking the "poetic diction" of the Eighteenth Century. For Pope and Wordsworth would doubtless each have held the other's poetic diction to be prosaic.

The value of Wordsworth's Prefaces has been too long hidden by discussions on the polemic validity of this and kindred sentences. Apart from these, the *Preface of 1800* marks an epoch in poetic criticism, and, with the *Essay, Supplementary to the Preface,* the *Preface to the Edition of 1815,* and Coleridge's *Biographia Literaria,* is the best introduction we have to the study of our century's poetry.

Wordsworth wrote opposite a passage from *Biographia Literaria* that he "never cared a straw about the theory." Knight's *Life,* Vol. II., p. 329.

[2] *Preface to the (first collected) Edition of Words-worth's Poems* (1815), where he distinguishes between and illustrates the literal, the fanciful, and the ima-ginative use of such words as "hang."

strange that even his friend Coleridge
misunderstood the dictum, for the poet
himself, in putting his theory into
practice, has occasionally followed the
erroneous, not the true, interpretation.
In such poems as *Alice Fell, The Idiot
Boy, Goody Blake and Harry Gill*, and
Peter Bell, Wordsworth's critics have
found the best argument both for their
interpretation and for their refutation of
his theory : in these the poet's attempt
to use the language of prose in poetry
has resulted in the prosaic use of language
in poetry, and his attempt to be simple
and natural has seduced him into an un-
natural simplicity.

A verse or two of *The Idiot Boy* will
prove this better than argument. Betty
Foy has a neighbour, Susan Gale, who
has taken suddenly unwell ; and, as
there is no one else at home, has to send
her idiot son on a pony for the doctor :

" And Betty's most especial charge
Was, ' Johnny ! Johnny ! mind that you
Come home again, nor stop at all,—

> Come home again, whate'er befall,
> My Johnny, do, I pray you do."

But after about thirty verses we find that Johnny has not come home again, nor has he reached his destination. The distress of poor Betty at the non-appearance of Johnny or doctor is then minutely described :

> "And Susan's growing worse and worse,
> And Betty's in a sad *quandary;*
> And then there's nobody to say
> If she must go, or she must stay !
> She's in a sad *quandary.*"

She at last resolves to leave poor Susan and to start off in search :

> " 'What can I do?' says Betty, going,
> 'What can I do to ease your pain?
> Good Susan, tell me, and I'll stay ;
> I fear you're in a dreadful way,
> But I shall soon be back again.' "
> .   .   .   .

> " So, through the moonlight lane she goes,
> And far into the moonlight dale ;
> And how she ran, and how she walked,
> And all that to herself she talked,
> Would surely be a tedious tale."

She ultimately arrives at the doctor's;
but no word of Johnny—

> " O Reader ! now that I might tell
> What Johnny and his Horse are doing,
> What they've been doing all this time,
> O could I put it into rhyme,
> A most delightful tale pursuing !"

We prefer to pursue it no further.
Suffice it to say that in the remaining
thirty verses or so, we find that Betty at
last finds her idiot boy astride the pony
that was so "mild and good," and that
to Betty's questions as to what he has
been doing in the moonlight "from eight
o'clock till five," he

> " Made answer, like a traveller bold,
> (His very words I give to you,)
> 'The cocks did crow to-whoo, to-whoo,
> And the sun did shine so cold !'
> —Thus answered Johnny in his glory,
> And that was all his travel's story."

The poet meant this poem to be
pathetic. The subject of our pathos is,
not its hero, but its author.[1]

---

[1] " Thus, when he tells the tale of Betty Foy,
     The idiot mother of 'an idiot boy ;'

Wordsworth writes that Burns' light, " breaking forth as nature's own "—

> " Showed my youth
> How verse may build a princely throne
> On humble truth."

We find in Burns the homeliest subjects and the homeliest language ; but we look in vain for futilities comparable to those so frequent in Wordsworth's ballads. Neither the success of *The Border Widow's Lament*, nor the failure of *The Idiot Boy* is to be traced to the *words* contained. Their difference is only superficially explained by even the contrast of the *use* of words ; for the root of Wordsworth's defect reaches deeper, to the imaginative conception. The materials of

---

A moon-struck, silly lad, who lost his way,
And, like his bard, confounded night with day ;
So close on each pathetic part he dwells,
And each adventure so sublimely tells,
That all who view the ' idiot in his glory,'
Conceive the bard the hero of the story."
　　—*English Bards and Scotch Reviewers.*

the poem have pathetic elements, which may therefore be made poetic. Wordsworth failed to make them poetic; and his failure is due to faults of commission as well as of omission. By emphasizing the vulgar accidents of morbid idiocy and maternal incapacity, he has obliterated the essential pathos in the workings of a mother's affections for her witless offspring. Wordsworth has given us an incongruous picture which from his lack of humour he did not recognize as burlesque.[1]

---

[1] Mr. Lowell expresses this succinctly: "Wordsworth never quite learned the distinction between Fact, which suffocates the Muse, and Truth, which is the very breath of her nostrils." *Among My Books.* Second Series, p. 226.

In Crabb Robinson's Diary, he says: "On my gently alluding to the line 'three feet long by two feet wide,' and confessing that I dared not read them aloud in company, he said, 'They ought to be liked !'"

His titles of his poems and constant references to the facts on which they were founded, are illustrations of the mixture of transcendentalism and realism which we find in his verse.

A few lines further on in his diary Crabb Robinson

Wordsworth's purpose in these "simple" poems was far from simple. All had a deep philosophic, if not poetic, intention ; though in most it is obscured, and in some hardly suggested.[1] Wordsworth's defence is in most of them more or less explicit. In *Simon Lee* he says :

"O Reader! had you in your mind
　　Such stores as silent thought can bring,
　O gentle Reader! you would find
　　A tale in everything." [2]

---

remarks : "Wordsworth, as Hazlitt has well observed, has a pride in deriving no aid from his subject. It is the mere power. which he is conscious of exerting, in which he delights. . . . In this as in other peculiarities of Wordsworth, there is a *German* bent in his mind."

[1] *Lucy Gray,* beautiful as well as "simple," is successful. But it also has this esoteric quality.

[2] Wordsworth's latest interpreter is evidently among those readers of Wordsworth who have failed to "find a tale in everything." Mr. John Morley, in his *Introduction* to *The Complete Poetical Works of William Wordsworth* (Macmillan, 1888), says: "It is best to be entirely sceptical as to the existence of system and ordered philosophy in Wordsworth. When

G

But the poet's function is to tell the "tale" for the reader who is not a Wordsworth. Were every man a poet there would be little need of poetry, for each "would find a tale in everything" for himself. The last verse of the *Anecdote for Fathers*—

> " O dearest, dearest Boy ! my heart
> For better love would seldom yearn,
> Could I but teach the hundredth part
> Of what from thee I learn,"—

is the poet's apology for leaving the reader with a conundrum which, though

---

he tells us that ' one impulse from a vernal wood may teach you more of man, of moral evil and of good, than all the sages can,' such a proposition cannot be seriously taken as more than a half-playful sally for the benefit of some too bookish friend. No impulse from a vernal wood can teach us anything at all of moral evil and of good " ! Scepticism as to the existence of a system does not preclude belief in the existence of thought in Wordsworth's poetry, still less of the deliberate thought which is part of the essence of Wordsworth's life and poetry ; and that the least playful of English poets treated it as no more than " a half-playful sally," is incredible.

soluble, is not solved by the prosaic sub-title, *Showing how the Practice of Lying may be Taught.* These poems are failures in so far as their "tale" is untold. The best of them contain materials for a poem ; some, materials for a sermon. The reader has to agree with Coleridge that " the *Anecdote for Fathers, Simon Lee, Alice Fell,* the *Beggars,* and the *Sailor's Mother,* not-withstanding the beauties which are to be found in each of them where the poet interposes the music of his own thoughts, would have been more delightful to me in prose, told and managed, as by Mr. Wordsworth they would have been in a moral essay or pedestrian tour."[1]

Putting aside this class of poems, we may now consider the criticisms that have been made on Wordsworth's pastorals and longer narrative pieces, and on the principle which guided him in their creation : that among the

---

[1] *Biographia Literaria*, chap. 18.

rustic and peasant classes we find the full development of the "essential passions" of mankind.

Wordsworth, in his tendency to what has been called "matter-of-factness," [1] has no doubt been too apt to regard his Michael, and Leech-Gatherer and Pedlar as portraits from life. And as a universal theory his statement is open to the objection which Coleridge makes: "I am convinced that for the human soul to prosper in rustic life a certain vantage-ground is pre-requisite. It is not every man that is likely to be improved by a country life or by country labours. Education, or original sensibility, or both, must pre-exist, if the changes, forms, and incidents of nature are to prove a sufficient stimulant." [2] Yet, as ideal pictures of what is natural and possible if the heart and intellect were duly trained under

---

[1] *Biographia Literaria*, chap. 22.
[2] *Biographia Literaria*, chap. 17.

Nature's influence apart from social culture and convention, the pastorals remain among the most essentially true and beautiful, as well as the most characteristic, of Wordsworth's poems. It is no argument against them to say that not one in a thousand of those from whom their characters are taken would appreciate a line of them, for the time may come when those ideals shall be facts, when our country-folk shall find in Nature, and perhaps in Wordsworth's poetry, a source of vital power and joy.

The valid objection against Wordsworth in this case lies in his limitation of his ideals to a single class—in his assumption that under the cultivating and refining influences of society we may not attain a still higher development of even "the essential passions" than is possible to rustic folk. The lady who has preserved her essential womanhood amid conventional restrictions, and developed it in a congenial and appropriate social atmosphere, is surely a more deeply natural product of humanity than is possible among the maids of even an ideal farmyard. The "essential passions" are not the monopoly of a class, though the narrow conventions of city life may do much to warp and dwarf them. The very temptations of refinement, education, and society, call out new powers of resistance; and in the moral equipoise of these we find an ideal with as much naturalness, and with much greater capability and play of "essential passions."

Esmond says: "'Tis an error, surely, to talk of the simplicity of youth. We get to understand truth better and therefore grow simpler as we grow older." Might we not transfer this saying to a comparison between the simplicity of Hodge and that of Dr. Johnson. We grow simpler and more natural as we grow wiser:

" For nature is made better by no mean,
But nature makes that mean. So over that art,
Which you say adds to nature, is an art

That nature makes. You see, sweet maid, we marry
A gentler scion to the wildest stock :
And make conceive a bark of baser kind
By bud of nobler race. This is an art
Which does mend nature—change it rather ; but
The art itself is nature."

Wordsworth's mental exclusiveness as a poet may be traced to his limitations as a man. We recall that scene of his youth, when, on his return from a country ball, as "magnificent the morning rose in memorable pomp," his "dedicated Spirit" found matter for reproach in the innocent enjoyment of "love-likings"; we recall his sonnets on *Personal Talk;* we realise the entire absence of humour, of dramatic power, of the more sensuous and tempestuous "essential passions," which makes so strongly against him in the affections of many. We think of what Chaucer and Shakespeare were, of what Goethe was, and are reminded of what Wordsworth was not.

Yet, after all, this limitation of Words-

worth's sympathies does not detract from
the truth and beauty of his best poetry.
It has a grandeur of its own, flowing from
the same springs as its defects. To set before us an ideal which might be possible
to all, is its "worthy purpose": a purpose for which the poet's individuality
was supremely fitted, and which has not
been achieved so perfectly by any poet
before or since. Wordsworth reminds
us of Milton in the solitary grandeur of
his verse, as in that of his character.[1]
To him, with even less reservation than
to Milton, might be applied his own line:

"Thy soul was like a star, and dwelt apart."

The moral and religious ideal is the inspiration of both. But Wordsworth is a
Milton of the nineteenth, not the seven-
teenth century. In place of a theological,
he has found a natural religion. Its revelation comes to him not so much from
above as from below and around.

"Love had he found in huts where poor men lie;
His daily teachers had been woods and rills,

The silence that is in the starry sky,
   The sleep that is among the lonely hills." [1]

The natural has become for him the supernatural. The wayside flowers, the clouds, the common joys, sorrows, and duties of every-day humanity, are transfigured in his verse, like the daffodils in his after-dream. In these he reads life's meaning, and to these he gives a freshness and a glory never given before. " He gives the charm of novelty to things of every day, and excites a feeling analogous to the supernatural, by awakening the mind's attention from the lethargy of custom, and directing it to the loveliness and the wonders of the world before us ; an inexhaustible treasure, but for which, in consequence of the film of familiarity and selfish solicitude, we have eyes, yet see not, ears that hear

---

[1] Coleridge is reported to have remarked of Wordsworth : " He is a man of whom it might have been said, ' It is good for him to be alone.' "

not, and hearts that neither feel nor understand." [1]

We cannot leave Wordsworth without a word on his poetic style. I do not refer to the theory on which he built his failures, but to the style in which his noblest poems were composed. Wordsworth, it may be, fell into a false, at times absurd, simplicity ; but the characteristic of his supreme work also is simplicity—a truer simplicity, in that it is the most natural possible to the poet and to

---

[1] *Biographia Literaria*, chap. 14. Compare Ruskin's words : "Wordsworth's distinctive work was a war with pomp and pretence, and a display of the majesty of simple feelings and humble hearts." *Modern Painters*, iii. 293. And Arnold's : "The cause of its greatness is simple, and may be told quite simply. Wordsworth's poetry is great because of the extraordinary power with which Wordsworth feels the joy offered to us in nature, the joy offered to us in the simple, primary affections and duties ; and because of the extraordinary power with which, in case after case, he shows us this joy, and renders it so as to make us share it." *Preface* to the *Selections*, p. 21.

his subject. Wordsworth's art may be
best compared to that of Nature.
" Nature herself seems," as Arnold says,
"to take the pen out of his hand, and
to write for him with her own bare,
sheer, penetrating power. . . . His
expression may often be called bald ;
. . . but it is bald as the bare mountain-
tops are bald, with a baldness which is
full of grandeur."[1] We look in vain
through his poems for anything that is
tricky or merely pretty. All is beauty,
unadorned by artifice. To illustrate
this simple, natural sublimity of Wordsworth's style, we may take his Sonnet
*Composed upon Westminster Bridge, Sept.
3, 1803.*

> " Earth has not anything to show more fair :
>   Dull would he be of soul who could pass by
>   A sight so touching in its majesty :
>   This City now doth, like a garment, wear
>   The beauty of the morning ; silent, bare,
>   Ships, towers, domes, theatres, and temples lie
>   Open unto the fields, and to the sky ;

---

[1] *Preface* to the *Selections*, p. 24.

All bright and glittering in the smokeless air.
Never did sun more beautifully steep
In his first splendour, valley, rock, or hill ;
Ne'er saw I, never felt, a calm so deep !
The river glideth at his own sweet will :
Dear God ! the very houses seem asleep ;
And all that mighty heart is lying still !"

Not a single heightening effect, not a single fanciful turn, to attract us or distract us : we are with Wordsworth on Westminster Bridge in the stillness of that autumn dawn and feel the solemnity he feels in the sight of the silent city lying all around.

Let us take leave of him listening to the singing of his country girl at work in one of our lonely Scottish glens :

" Behold her, single in the field,
    Yon solitary Highland Lass !
    Reaping and singing by herself ;
    Stop here, or gently pass !
    Alone she cuts and binds the grain,
    And sings a melancholy strain ;
    O listen ! for the Vale profound
    Is overflowing with the sound.

" No Nightingale did ever chaunt
    So sweetly to reposing bands

Of Travellers in some shady haunt,
Among Arabian sands:
A voice so thrilling ne'er was heard
In spring-time from the Cuckoo-bird,
Breaking the silence of the seas
Among the farthest Hebrides.

" Will no one tell me what she sings?—
Perhaps the plaintive numbers flow
For old, unhappy, far-off things,
And battles long ago:
Or is it some more humble lay,
Familiar matter of to-day?
Some natural sorrow, loss, or pain,
That has been, and may be again?"

" Whate'er the theme, the Maiden sang
As if her song could have no ending;
I saw her singing at her work,
And o'er the sickle bending;—
I listened till I had my fill,
And when I mounted up the hill,
The music in my heart I bore,
Long after it was heard no more."

Yet Wordsworth is not popular. Perhaps it is—besides his limitations, which I have already emphasized enough—that we do not become intimate either with our best poets or with our best friends at a first or second meeting. The most

genuine and sincere do not flaunt their
best qualities in our faces, and often fail
to attract us at first sight. They make
no advances. They are reserved. To
know them, to become intimate with
them, is difficult ; but the difficulty is
usually proportionate to the value of their
acquaintance. Wordsworth has said of
another,

> "You must love him, ere to you
>   He will seem worthy of your love ; "

but the lines are most appropriate of all
to himself.

Wordsworth is not easy reading; for
he does not accentuate his points or make
a show of his emotions for the running
reader.   The difficulty lies in his simplicity.   We have to dismiss our cleverness, and read him "like a little child."
After all, we should not be too sure we
understand him fully, for he addresses
the understanding through the heart,[1]

---

[1] Compare his own account in *The Prelude*, book
xi., of the influence of Nature and of his Sister, which

and is thus in danger of being misunderstood alike by the vulgar and by the learned.

For this reason, an appreciation of Wordsworth is likelier to afford a sure foundation of taste than that of any other of our modern poets. Quite apart from his greatness in comparison with others, an appreciation of his work among those of us who are forming our poetical taste is preferable, as a beginning, to an appreciation of Byron, or of Shelley, or of Browning: it is preferable because it is less likely to be false—to be an appreciation merely of what is accidental.

The splendid revolt of Shelley, or the somewhat bizarre melancholy of Byron, finds a sympathetic chord in young readers, quite apart from the real meaning of either—the cause or purpose of

---

"led him back through opening day
To those sweet counsels between head and heart
Whence grew that genuine knowledge, fraught with peace."

either—which is the essential part of it. Or again, our cleverness gets a proper field for its display in making grammar and sense out of Browning, quite apart from the question whether the sense found were worth our ingenuity. Not that there is no more than revolt, and melancholy, and obscurity in these poets. But we may easily rest satisfied with the accidental trappings or phases which first take our fancy, and never reach the vital ideas underlying these in each. Because we are melancholy and we find Byron is melancholy, we may fancy we have a thorough understanding of Byron, when our melancholy and his may be entirely different in cause and meaning. And so with Browning's cleverness and ours. Are we certain that we do not frequently mistake obscurity for depth, and that, while we think we are plumbing an ocean, we are not puddling among grammatical and psychological shallows? An even ardent appreciation of these poets may not be the true one ; for it may be an understanding of, and sympathy with, accidentals, rather than with essentials.

But in reading Wordsworth, such a self-deception is unlikely ; for his poetry has no accidental attractions to allure us by superficial sympathies. Indeed, any evident qualities his poetry possesses are at first rather repellant than attractive : they make not for him but against him in his way to our appreciation. And, therefore, what taste we do form by study of him is sure to be thorough, a permanent possession.

The self-centred calm of Wordsworth is not the atmosphere of youth's generous and adventurous aspirations. The mature flavour of reflective cheerfulness which seasons his poetry, and his austere plainness of subject, of thought and of style, are tasteless alike to the uninitiated and to the jaded appetite. Not a subject of his that is not at first view commonplace ; not a phrase that at first hearing titillates our passing fancy by its cleverness or high - strung passion. Yet Wordsworth's simplicity, his commonplace, like Nature's, has a depth and a beauty of its own ; and if we love it, we love it for itself. "Type of the wise who soar, but never roam ; true to the kindred points of heaven and home," he sings to us " of joy in widest commonalty spread"; and, if we can but attune our ears, we will feel " Wordsworth's healing power."

Browning.

Browning.

————◆————

MODESTY is a characteristic of neither
travellers nor critics. There are few things
which the former have not seen, or which
the latter have not understood. Yet our
mediæval traveller, Mandeville, was not
more despairing when he came to talk
of Paradise, than were the critics of last
generation when their subject was the
poetry of Robert Browning. Some of
you may remember Mandeville's description of the obstacles that barred
"man that is mortal" from a sight of
Paradise, which, "as I have heard say of
wise men," "is far beyond." "For by
land no man may go for wild beasts, that
are in the deserts, and for the high

mountains, and great huge rocks that no man may pass by for the dark places that are there ; and by the rivers may no man go. Many died for weariness of rowing against the strong waves ; and many became blind, and many deaf, for the noise of the water ; and some perished and were lost in the waves ; so that no mortal may approach to that place without special grace of God ; so that of that place I can tell you no more." Twenty years ago this might have been an allegory of most criticisms of Browning's poetry. To-day all is changed. Patience and science have done much. Mountains have become plains, rocks have been blasted, electric light has dispelled the darkness, and the deserts have burst into flower and fruit. For one weary pilgrim there are a thousand jaunty travellers. Fifty societies are plying excursion-parties up the formerly impassable streams.

Yet, if one difficulty has been solved, another has taken its place. Critics

now pause not so much before the
obscurity and harshness of Browning's
poetry, as before its amount. In 1868
his works filled six volumes ; to-day,
they are about to be published in
sixteen. As the garrulity of age is a
common-place as well of genius as of
mediocrity, the number in the final
edition remains indefinite. At present
he is the most prolific of modern English
poets.

It is clear that the interpretation of
Browning must be suggestive rather
than exhaustive. I will attempt merely
to indicate the main features of his
genius by a few examples.

"Mr. Browning's paternal grandfather
was an Englishman of a west country
stock ; his paternal grandmother a
Creole. The maternal grandfather was
a German from Hamburg named
Wiedemann, an accomplished draughts-
man and musician. The maternal
grandmother was completely Scotch."

These hereditary influences, and a

long residence in Italy, partly explain
the luxurious and vigorous growth of the
poet's genius. With independent means,
he was from the first free to devote his
time and energies to poetry. *Pauline*
was published when he was a boy of
twenty ; *Paracelsus* followed within two,
Sordello within seven years. These
works display, more or less, immaturity.
They are written "according to a scheme
too extravagant and scale too impracti-
cable" for poetic art. The method is, as
in all his poetry, introspective ; but the
introspection is as much that of autobio-
graphy as that of drama. "The thing,"
says Browning of *Pauline*, "was my
earliest attempt at 'poetry always
dramatic in principle, and so many
utterances of so many imaginary
persons, not mine.'" Yet the reader
recognises in the three poems the over-
ambition and impatience of a genius
whose enthusiasm has not yet been
tempered into judgment by experience.
They are partly "confessions" of the

self-consciousness, at times almost mor-
bidity, of youth, before the soul has
realised and adjusted itself to limits.
In this respect they contrast with the
work of the author's genial maturity.
Save in occasional passages in *Sordello*,
the author's characteristic humour is
absent ; yet the germs of his genius may
be traced : his appetite for belief, his
devotion to art, and his analytic insight
into character. All his after-works, as
Sordello, treat of " incidents in the development of a human soul." He trans-
lates and exalts

" The proper study of mankind is man."

Browning's Dramas, extending from
Strafford, three years before *Sordello*, to
Luria and *A Soul's Tragedy*, in 1846,
and interrupted by the publication of
his Dramatic Lyrics and Romances,
mark the second period in the development of his genius. Some have been
successfully produced : none has kept
the stage. Yet they are neither obscure,

nor wanting in incident—even sensa-
tional incident. They are not generally
popular, because they lack scenic situation, and fail to appeal to the ordinary
interests of our theatre-going public.
Of the dramas, *Colombe's Birthday* is the
most pleasant and simple reading ; *A
Blot on the 'Scutcheon* is the best fitted
for dramatic representation.

For illustration, *Pippa Passes* may be
chosen, as the most characteristic and
most varied.

Pippa is a young factory girl who
works in the silk-mills of Asolo. It is
New Year's Day, her only holiday. In
the opening scene, she springs from bed
at sunrise, resolved to enjoy herself to
the full : she will not " squander a wave-
let," not "a mite of her twelve hours'
treasure." She has but this one day.
Others in Asolo may be happy the
whole year through. Ottima, her em-
ployer's wife, with her lover Sebald's
homage : Jules, the artist—this is his
wedding-day : Luigi, the young revolu-

tionary enthusiast, who has a mother's devotion: and the great Monsignor who has just arrived from Rome to say masses for his brother's soul:—these "Four Happiest Ones" she thinks of and envies for a moment. Yet she reflects that after all God's love is best.

" Now wait !—even I already seem to share
  In God's love: what does New-year's hymn declare?
  What other meaning do these verses bear?
    All service ranks the same with God:
    If now, as formerly he trod
    Paradise, his presence fills
    Our earth, each only as God wills
    Can work—God's puppets, best and worst,
    Are we; there is no last nor first.

   .   .   .   .

And more of it, and more of it !—oh yes—
I will pass each, and see their happiness,
And envy none—being just as great, no doubt,
Useful to men, and dear to God, as they !
A pretty thing to care about
So mightily, this single holiday !
But let the sun shine ! wherefore repine?
—With thee to lead me, O Day of mine,
Down the grass path grey with dew,
Under the pine-wood, blind with boughs,
Where the swallow never flew
Nor yet cicala dared carouse—
No, dared carouse !   [*She enters the street.*"

Pippa's hymn is the text of the drama; her singing, as she passes Asolo's Four Happiest Ones is the connecting thread of the following Parts, which are little more than independent Scenes, each revealing an intense and critical moment in a life.

In the first Part, Ottima, the silk-spinner's wife, is with her lover, Sebald, on the morning after her husband's murder. With 'the blood-red beam through the shutter's chink,' there come to Sebald remembrance and remorse.

"Morning?
It seems to me a night with a sun added.
Where's dew, where's freshness? That bruised plant, I bruised
In getting through the lattice yestereve,
Droops as it did. See, here's my elbow's mark
I' the dust o' the sill.

Ottima.   Oh, shut the lattice, pray !

Sebald. Let me lean out. I cannot scent blood here,
Foul as the morn be.
                    There, shut the world out !
How do you feel now, Ottima ? There, curse
The world and all outside ! Let us throw off

This mask : how do you bear yourself? Let's out
With all of it."

Ottima, absorbed in her passion, tries to
drown his thought—with wine, with
diversion to other themes, with reminiscences of their passionate past. For a
moment she succeeds.

Ottima. Buried in woods we lay, you recollect ;
Swift ran the scorching tempest overhead ;
And ever and anon some bright white shaft
Burned thro' the pine-tree roof, here burned and
  there,
As if God's messenger thro' the close wood screen
Plunged and replunged his weapon at a venture,
Feeling for guilty thee and me : then broke
The thunder like a whole sea overhead—

Sebald. Yes !

 . . . .

 I kiss you now, dear Ottima, now and now !
This way ? Will you forgive me—be once more
My great queen ?

Ottima.   Bind it thrice about my brow ;
Crown me your queen, your spirit's arbitress,
Magnificent in sin. Say that !

Sebald.   I crown you
My great white queen, my spirit's arbitress,
Magnificent . . .

[From without is heard the voice of PIPPA, *singing—*

The year's at the spring
And day's at the morn ;
Morning's at seven ;
The hill-side's dew-pearled ;
The lark's on the wing ;
The snail's on the thorn :
God's in his heaven—
All's right with the world !

[PIPPA *passes.*

Sebald.   God's in his heaven !   Do you hear
   that ?   Who spoke ?
You, you spoke !

Ottima.   Oh—that little ragged girl !
She must have rested on the step : we give them
But this one holiday the whole year round.
Did you ever see our silk-mills—their inside ?
There are ten silk-mills now belong to you.
She stoops to pick my double heartsease . . . Sh !"

But passion and guilt have lost the field.

Sebald.   " My God, and she is emptied of it
   now !
Outright now !—how miraculously gone
All of the grace—had she not strange grace once ? "

In the end the conscience of the man,
and the heart of the woman, are vic-
torious over death.

The second Part presents us with

"another way of love." Jules is the
victim of a plot devised by his brother
artists. They have led him to marry a
peasant girl whom he believes from a
feigned correspondence to be a cultured
lady; and he is leaving her with revenge
on his enemies in his heart, when Pippa
passes and her singing again solves a
crisis. Her song, of " Kate the Queen "
who was beloved by her page, lures his
thoughts into a fresh channel.

> " If whoever loves
> Must be, in some sort, god or worshipper,
> The blessing or the blest one, queen or page,
> Why should we always choose the page's part ?
> Here is a woman with utter need of me, —
> I find myself queen here, it seems !
>   How strange !
> Look at the woman here with the new soul,
> Like my own Psyche,—fresh upon her lips
> Alit, the visionary butterfly,
> Waiting my word to enter and make bright,
> Or flutter off and leave all blank as first . . .
> Shall to produce form out of unshaped stuff
> Be Art—and further, to evoke a soul
> From form be nothing ? This new soul is mine !"

Pygmalion finds a soul in himself as

well as in his bride.　A spark from Pippa's song reveals the egotism of his life and work.　He breaks his " paltry models up to begin Art afresh," and plans a nobler revenge for his enemy, Lutwyche, in—

" Some unsuspected isle in the far seas ! "

Patriotic passion is the subject of the third Part ; and its moral is one of the author's favourite texts,

" The unlit lamp and the ungirt loin ! " [1]

A mother is reasoning with her son at sunset in the Turret on the Hill, and has almost persuaded him to relinquish for a personal love, a noble, because nobly meant, self-sacrifice in his country's cause, when the chords of Pippa's song rouse the political enthusiast from his infirmity, and he rushes off to achieve his end and save his honour.

The fourth and last Part introduces

---

[1] *The Statue and the Bust.*

the meagre plot that holds the play together. The great Monsignor and his Intendant are discovered conversing in the Palace by the Duomo. Unknown to Pippa, the man whom she has revered and envied as " the holy and beloved priest " is her wicked uncle. She is the only child of an elder brother at whose death Monsignor has connived. Pippa is the one obstacle to his enjoyment of her father's wealth ; and a plan is being laid before him by the Intendant for her ruin, when Pippa passes. Again some note in her pure song converts a soul. Springing up, he has summoned his people to " gag this villain—tie him hand and foot " before the curtain falls on his " *Miserere mei, Domine.*"

The play concludes, as it opened, with a scene in Pippa's chamber, where we find her, home again at sunset, thoughtful over her day's experiences.

Now, one thing I should really like to know :
How near I ever might approach all these
I only fancied being, this long day :

I

—Approach, I mean, so as to touch them, so
As to . . . in some way . . . move them—
    if you please,
Do good or evil to them some slight way.
For instance, if I wind
Silk to-morrow, my silk may bind
                    [Sitting on the bedside.
And border Ottima's cloak's hem.
Ah me, and my important part with them,
This morning's hymn half promised when I rose !
True in some sense or other, I suppose.
                    [As she lies down.
God bless me ! I can pray no more to-night,
No doubt, some way or other, hymns say right.
    All service ranks the same with God—
    With God, whose puppets, best and worst,
    Are we : there is no last nor first.
                    [She sleeps.

I have left unnoticed the Scene between each part—the two first in verse, the third in prose—which admirably illustrate the author's power of pathos and of half-grotesque humour, and which serve to cement the parts together.

Enough has been given, to show that this work is not a drama in the orthodox sense. It is built, not woven : the intermediate scenes are but

mortar between the stones of a parti-
coloured column. The Parts are essentially independent dramatic studies,
bound together by a series of applica-
tions of a text.

As another illustration of the drift of
Browning's method in his maturer work,
we might take *A Soul's Tragedy*, in
which the interest is almost entirely
centred in soliloquy. A shorter piece
will serve our purpose. *In a Balcony*, in
which the dramatist himself has recognised that the part is better than the
whole, has a unity which many of his complete dramas lack. There are but three
characters and one Scene. The lovers,
Norbert and Constance, are together on
the balcony of the Palace : the one, a
successful statesman, the other, a cousin
and dependant, of the Queen who is
this night holding a royal reception in
honour of Norbert's political success.
The lover wishes to claim his bride from
the Queen, as the reward of his service.
But Constance, from her knowledge of

her cousin, fears for the result, and at
last with difficulty persuades him to ask
the favour indirectly as a subtle flattery.
The solitary, heart-starved Queen has re-
ceived and mistaken Norbert's proposal
as one for her own hand, when she
enters to tell Constance of her joy. Constance realises gradually her situation,
and with woman-like self-sacrifice braces
herself to resign her lover to one who
loves him with the passion of a long-
thwarted nature. When Norbert enters
to claim his reward, we are able to
realise the intensity of the climax which
the dramatist has chosen for one of his
subtlest revelations of character.

The method in this "Fragment" is
characteristic.[1] The purpose of con-
structing a unity out of diverse elements,
or of presenting the development of the
characters of his *dramatis personæ*

---

[1] From first to last, his dramas are studies '' of
Action in Character, rather than Character in Action.'
—*Preface to Strafford* (1837).

through scenic situation, is sacrificed more and more to his main intention of revealing the secret recesses of individual souls. The critical moment in which the soul is seen at its fullest is of supreme interest to him ; the rest is subsidiary. *Pippa Passes* is but four moments chosen for the microscopic revelation of five " human souls" : *In a Balcony*, a scene in which the dramatist catches three souls at their intensest life.

Thus it is but a step from Browning's dramas to his dramatic lyrics and romances. To the reader of his dramas the question constantly occurs : What the need of accessories at all, or of binding independent scenes together by comparatively irrelevant details? "Why such long prolusion and display?" Four years before the last of his dramas the author himself had answered the question by the publication of *Dramatic Lyrics* (1842). This volume was followed by *Dramatic Romances and Lyrics* (1845), *Men and Women* (1855), and *Dramatis*

Personæ (1864), the similarity of method in which marks the third period in his genius.   This method was more or less a return from his attempts at

" The simulation of the painted scene,
      Boards, actors, prompters, gaslight, and costume "

to that in *Paracelsus.*   But the author has matured his dramatic treatment by realizing its essential limitations.   As in *Paracelsus*, "instead of having recourse to an external machinery of incidents to create and evolve the crisis," he has "suffered the agency by which it is influenced and determined, to be generally discernible in its effects alone, and subordinate throughout, if not altogether excluded."   But in his *Dramatic Lyrics* the dramatist has found it expedient to reduce his canvas, and to attempt the "minute display" not of a series of pictures, but of one.   In these four volumes the microscopic lens of Browning's imagination has found its focus.   It is needless to take them separately; it would be idle to classify poems of such varied subject and purpose.[1] Yet it is well to illustrate their most marked variations of form and conception.

My Last Duchess is the first of the author's " monologues " : though eclipsed by some, such as *Fra Lippo Lippi* and *Andrea del Sarto*, in interest and scope of subject, it is typical of all. Like the separate scenes of his former work, this piece is a momentary study which has yet brought every minute trait into a strong relief. But it is set alone, a unity within itself ; preliminary introduction to the person or the situation is dispensed with ; and the actor is left to reveal himself. Dramatic action and accessory are reduced to their barest limits. Who is the speaker, and what are the circumstances, are questions the answer

---

[1] The vagueness of the distinction between Lyric and Romance is evident from the fact that the author himself has in later editions transferred pieces from one class to the other.

to which must be gathered from the speech. A first reading will reveal that " A widowed Duke of Ferrara is exhibiting the portrait of his former wife, to the envoy of some nobleman, whose daughter he proposes to marry." A deeper reading will be requisite to realize that it is a minute and masterly creation of "a typical autocrat of the Renaissance, with his serene self-composure of selfishness, quiet, uncompromising cruelty, and genuine devotion to art."

Of the author's originality of dramatic conception and method in these volumes, this example is but a general type. Every piece is a variation, ranging from passion to reflection, from argument to narrative. Some are soliloquies rather than speeches ; some, songs rather than soliloquies ; others, simple stories simply told. The monologue serves in one to recall a drama, in another to discuss a problem, in a third to catch a mood. Yet, however varied the process, each contains a soul " under

lock and key"; each is, as it were, the
plate of a camera, which developes to
its minutest detail, before our eyes. The
variety in subject of these poems is as
marvellous as that in their conception;
and each piece has a rhythm and
rhyme of its own. Love is a province in every recess of which Browning has asserted supremacy. The
reader turns from the measured cadence
of *Evelyn Hope* to the warble of *My
Star*, from the half-humourous, half-
pathetic rhymes of *Youth and Art* to the
grave melody of *The Worst of It.* The
ferocity of the *Soliloquy of the Spanish
Cloister* and *The Confessional* are equally
within the poet's compass, with the mis-
understandings of *A Lover's Quarrel*
and the reflective calm of *By the Fireside.*
The characteristic of all is that they are
dramatic. Each is the minute imaginative transcript, not of an abstract feeling,
but of an individual mood.

Many of the shorter lyrics, as *Home
Thoughts from Abroad* and *The Eng-*

lishman in Italy, are little more than pictures of nature ; yet the description is always made to reflect the mood ; it never loses its dramatic quality. The scene in *Love among the Ruins* :—

> " Where the quiet-coloured end of evening smiles,
> Miles and miles
> On the solitary pastures where our sheep
> Half-asleep
> Tinkle homeward thro' the twilight, stray or stop
> As they crop "—

is not a mere setting, but an essential part of the portrait. Or take for another example the following passage from *Saul*, where David blends his spirit and the fields around him into music—

> " Then I tuned my harp,—took off the lilies we twine
> round its chords
> Lest they snap 'neath the stress of the noontide—those
> sunbeams like swords !
> And I first played the tune all our sheep know, as, one
> after one,
> So docile they come to the pen-door till folding be
> done.
> They are white and untorn by the bushes, for lo, they
> have fed
> Where the long grasses stifle the water within the
> stream's bed ;

And now one after one seeks its lodging, as star
    follows star
Into eve and the blue far above us,—so blue and so
    far ! "

This dramatic method was adapted to other purposes than individual portraiture; purposes which, though for the most part secondary in those four volumes, have in his later work a more and more prominent place, viz., the presentation of historical pictures and of philosophic and didactic argument. Even the first of the poet's shorter pieces—*My Last Duchess, Count Gismond*, and the *Soliloquy of the Spanish Cloister*—are each a picture not only of an individual or a mood, but of an age and nation. These were followed by a series of historical studies, taken from almost every nationality and period of importance in the past, and extending from the first Hebrew king to a Catholic bishop of our time. Of mediaeval Florence we have *Fra Lippo Lippi* and *Andrea del Sarto ;* of Venice in her decline, *A Toccata of Galuppi's ;* of the first Christian century, *Cleon, An Epistle of Karshish* and *A Death on the Desert ;* of the Middle-Ages and Renaissance, *The Bishop orders his Tomb at St. Praxed's Church, A Grammarian's Funeral,* and *Holy Cross Day.* In some the interest is in the character, in others it is centred in the history, in all we discover the exceptional scope and accuracy of the scholar's learning as of the poet's imagination. In many of the above poems, the conception is not only historical but philosophical.

From *Pauline* to *Parleyings with Certain People,* the metaphysics of religion and art has had over the poet an equal fascination with that of history. The subject of *Sordello* and *Paracelsus* is more philosophical than dramatic. In the work of his maturer years we find the author applying more and more frequently his monologue to dramatic exposition of problems. The first two volumes of his *Lyrics and Romances* do not reveal this ; but *Christmas Eve and Easter Day*, published in 1850, is an avowed study in the philosophy of religion. *Men and Women*, which followed five years after, contains one or two pieces, such as *The Statue and the Bust, A Grammarian's Funeral, Popularity*, and *Transcendentalism*, which are openly didactic, a few which are each a study in character, history, and philosophy in one, as *An Epistle of Karshish, Cleon*, and *Saul.* In *Dramatis Personæ* (1864), the majority of the pieces are critical and metaphysical. *Mr. Sludge the Medium* is a companion study in casuistry to *Bishop Blougram's Apology ; Abt Vogler, Rabbi ben Ezra, A Death in the Desert*, and *Caliban upon Setebos*, are philosophy dramatically presented ; and each narrative piece has a moral, though not always expressed.

The later volumes of the poet's shorter pieces, *Pacchiarotto, with other Poems* (1876), *Dramatic Idyls* (1880), *Jocoseria* (1883), *Ferishtah's Fancies* (1884), and

Parleyings with Certain People (1887),
are evidence of the poet's lyric and dramatic fertility ; but in variety of subject
and method they differ only slightly
from the specimens already named ; and
there may be traced in their dramatic
treatment an increasing tendency to
sacrifice the study of character to that of
artistic, philosophic, or religious problems. In his two last volumes, the dramatist is swallowed up in the scholiast :
the one is a collection of allegories in
Persian dress with lyrical interpretations,
the other a series of metaphysical discussions on religion, science, and art.

Since *The Ring and the Book* (1868),
Browning has published other longer
works. *Balaustion's Adventure* (1871),
Aristophanes' Apology (1875), and *The
Agamemnon* (1877), are studies from the
Greek of Euripides and Æschylus, and
contain translations which are astonish-
ing for their literal perfection. *The Inn
Album* (1875), *The Two Poets of Croisic*
(1878), *Prince Hohenstiel - Schwangau*

(1871), *Fifine at the Fair* (1872), and
Red Cotton Night-cap Country (1873),
are studies in narrative based on facts,
characteristic of Browning's involved
and subtle treatment ; the first two are
comparatively simple reading. *La Sai-
siaz* (1878), which has an even slighter
dramatic setting than *Christmas Eve*,
and is a purely philosophic poem on
immortality, exhausts the catalogue of
the poet's works, since the publication of
his masterpiece.

The Ring and the Book marks the
crest of the wave of Browning's genius.
It is the crowning evidence of the dramatist's originality of style. He has here
found a subject for a larger canvas than
that of his former monologues, yet
demanding essentially the same treatment. A critical analysis is outside our
purpose which will be served by an
indication of the plan of the work. The
first of the twelve Books tells the story,
" a mere Roman murder case," in full
detail, showing clearly the bearing and

consequence of each event, as well as
the right and wrong of each *dramatis
persona.* The poet thus shows us at the
outset that his purpose is not to tell a
story. Here are the bare facts :—

"Count Guido Franceschini the Aretine,
Descended of an ancient house, though poor,
A beak-nosed, bushy-bearded, black-haired lord,
Lean, pallid, low of stature yet robust,
Fifty years old,—having four years ago
Married Pompilia Comparini, young,
Good, beautiful, at Rome, where she was born,
And brought her to Arezzo, where they lived
Unhappy lives, whatever curse the cause,—
This husband, taking four accomplices,
Followed this wife to Rome, where she was fled
From their Arezzo to find peace again,
In convoy, eight months earlier, of a priest,
Aretine also, of still nobler birth,
Giuseppe Caponsacchi,—caught her there
Quiet in a villa on a Christmas night,
With only Pietro and Violante by,
Both her putative parents ; killed the three,
Aged, they, seventy each, and she, seventeen,
And, two weeks since, the mother of his babe
First born and heir to what the style was worth
O' the Guido who determined, dared and did
This deed just as he purposed point by point.
Then, bent upon escape, but hotly pressed,

And captured with his co-mates that same night,
He, brought to trial, stood on this defence—
Injury to his honour caused the act ;
And since his wife was false, (as manifest
By flight from home in such companionship,)
Death, punishment deserved of the false wife
And faithless parents who abetted her
I' the flight aforesaid, wronged nor God nor man.
' Nor false she, nor yet faithless they,' replied
The accuser ; 'cloaked and masked this murder glooms ;
' True was Pompilia, loyal too the pair ;
' Out of the man's own heart a monster curled
' Which crime coiled with connivancy at crime—
' His victim's breast, he tells you, hatched and reared ;
' Uncoil we and stretch stark the worm of hell ! '
A month the trial swayed this way and that
Ere judgment settled down on Guido's guilt ;
Then was the Pope, that good Twelfth Innocent,
Appealed to : who well weighed what went before,
Affirmed the guilt and gave the guilty doom."

This narrative is but a key by which
the dramatist proposes to unlock the
recesses of nine souls ; and he proceeds
to do this by ten monologues, in each
of which a character tells his version
of the story. The second, third, and
fourth books represent the views of the
public of Rome : two of them, " Half-

K

Rome" and "The Other Half-Rome,"
taking opposite sides, equally inconclu-
sive, and the third, "Tertium Quid," re-
presenting the aristocratic impartiality
of indifference.   In the next three monologues, the persons of the drama bear
witness of themselves, Count Guido and
Caponsacchi before the court, Pompilia
on her deathbed.   The two following
books reveal the lawyers on each side,
engaged in the composition of their re-
spective statements of the case.   Then
comes the memorable soliloquy of the
Pope, to whom the case has been referred
for judgment ; next we listen to Guido's
second monologue on the night before
his death.   The last book, like the first,
contains the author's narrative, which
completes the whole by gathering up
the different threads and relating Guido's
execution.   The poet adds to this, as to
the first book, a lyric addressed to his
wife, over whom the grave had closed.

This is a bare statement of the plan of
Browning's masterpiece, which marshals

in a splendid phalanx all the great
qualities scattered throughout his preceding work,—yet a masterpiece marred
by the appearance of a Falstaff's "ragged
regiment" of quaint puerilities, ingeni-
ously stupid conceits, and unfathomable
nonsense. The stream of Browning's
genius is constantly overflowing its banks
and stagnating in marshes. Of his tendency to grotesqueness we saw an indication as far back as *Pippa Passes;* but
the pranks which his supersubtlety plays
through the mouths of the two lawyers,
with their rudimentary Latin and nonde-
script inanities, come upon us with a
shock. As Landor pointed out fifty years
ago, the poet's lynx-eyed vision sees
every possible aspect of the human problem which it views. His characteristic
error is in attempting to see too much,
in peering and botanizing, or in imagin-
ing impossible fourth dimensions. This
is the genesis of that grotesqueness,
which, like the "canker in the fairest

bud," takes most definite shape in his greatest work.

In the work of an artist like Tennyson, we see the picture, and the picture alone. In that of Browning, we see each stroke of the brush and mark of the thumb, the very net-work of his canvas. He inserts everything : he puts all his notes into the text. In the *Idylls of the King* we have the wine of the grapes ; in *The Ring and the Book*, twelve baskets-full of leaves and fruit.

Browning's interest in everything is as intense as Nature's ; and, when inspired, he works like Nature herself. His three greatest exhibitions of this power are Pompilia, Caponsacchi, and the Pope. It is scarcely less manifest in the presentation of Count Guido Franceschini, a villain with the cunning of Iago, the cowardness and meanness of Jonas Chuzzlewit. To find a parallel for Pompilia we must go beyond fiction. More than the devout Catholic imagines of goodness, of womanhood, of tenderness

made divine by sorrow, in the Virgin
Mother, is realized in her. Of Caponsacchi, Pompilia's "soldier-saint," with
"the broad brow that reverberates the
truth," what praise is needed more than
this,—that she would have sprung to his
"great heart" and "strong hand,"

> "beckoning across
> Murder and hell gigantic and distinct
> O' the threshold, posted to exclude me heaven."

In the Pope, the old man who stands
awestruck and trembling, but faithful
and strong, between heaven and hell, to
whom every moment is the Judgment-
Day, who looks upon himself as the conscience of the world, we have the most
complete revelation of Browning's genius.
All the resources of his learning are with
apparent spontaneity brought to the service of his fancy. The blank verse peals
and lightens : the poet wields it like Thor
smiting icebergs with his hammer. His
analytic power is here transformed into
intuition. No soul that has communed

with destiny since Shakspeare's spirit brooded on the world, has so divided light from darkness, distilled evil from good, and "vindicated the ways of God to man," as Browning has in the greatest poem of the twelve that make up *The Ring and the Book.*

> " I stood at Naples once, a night so dark
> I could have scarce conjectured there was earth
> Anywhere, sky or sea or world at all :
> But the night's black was burst through by a blaze —
> Thunder struck blow on blow, earth groaned and
>   bore,
> Through her whole length of mountain visible :
> There lay the city thick and plain with spires,
> And, like a ghost disshrouded, white the sea.
> So may the truth be flashed out by one blow,
> And Guido see, one instant, and be saved.
> Else I avert my face, nor follow him
> Into that sad obscure sequestered state
> Where God unmakes but to remake the soul
> He else made first in vain ; which must not be.
> Enough, for I may die this very night
> And how should I dare die, this man let live ?
>
> Carry this forthwith to the Governor ! "

Introduction to the uninitiated reader is in this work less called for than in the

shorter pieces; for the poet himself supplies it. Many, therefore, to whom his
Dramatic Lyrics are mere perplexities,
will find here little difficulty.

It is difficult to give any adequate
idea of Browning's style; for he has all
styles. In variety of rhythm and fertility
of rhyme he is among English poets un-
surpassed. The metre of each poem is an
essential part of its conception; he turns
with almost provoking rapidity from lyric
to narrative, from passion to reflection,
from the swiftness of a crisis to the
casuistry of an argument.

As an illustration of the lyrist's melody,
take Mertoun's song [1]:—

" There's a woman like a dew-drop, she's so purer
    than the purest ;
  And her noble heart's the noblest, yes, and her
    sure faith's the surest :
  And her eyes are dark and humid, like the depth
    on depth of lustre
  Hid i' the harebell, while her tresses, sunnier than
    the wild-grape cluster,

---

[1] *A Blot in the 'Scutcheon,* Act I., Scene 3.

Gush in golden-tinted plenty down her neck's rose-
    misted marble ;
Then her voice's music . . . call it the well's
    bubbling, the bird's warble !

And this woman says, ' My days were sunless and
    my nights were moonless,
' Parched the pleasant April herbage, and the lark's
    heart's outbreak tuneless,
' If you loved me not ! ' And I who—(ah, for words
    of flame !) adore her,
Who am mad to lay my spirit prostrate palpably
    before her—
I may enter at her portal soon, as now her lattice
    takes me,
And by noontide as by midnight make her mine,
    as hers she makes me ! "

Or turn to these lines in *James Lee's Wife*, which the lapping sea sets to its music :—

  " Oh, good gigantic smile o' the brown old earth,
     This autumn morning ! How he sets his bones
    To bask i' the sun, and thrusts out knees and feet
    For the ripple to run over in its mirth ;
     Listening the while, where on the heap of stones
    The white breast of the sea-lark twitters sweet."

The reader of either volume of the poet's *Selections* will find a fresh accent in every poem. The organ-notes of *Abt Vogler*, the march of the *Cavalier Tunes*, the hand-gallop of *Through the Metidja to Abd-el-Kadr*, show a mastery over metre as remarkable as the variety in the blank verse of Fra Lippo Lippi, of Andrea del Sarto, of Bishop Blougram, and of Sludge.[1] In his pride of strength the poet at times seems to make his task purposely difficult. Like a Japanese acrobat he dances under a heavy weight. In many pieces his grotesque humour finds vent in the double jingle of eccentric, sometimes preposterous rhymes, as in *Youth and Art*—

" We studied hard in our styles,
    Chipped each a crust like Hindoos,
For air looked out on the tiles,
    For fun watched each other's windows. . .

" No harm ! It was not my fault
    If you never turned your eye's tail up
As I shook upon E *in alt*,
    Or ran the chromatic scale up : . . .

---

[1] Compare also the varieties in the blank verse of the different monologues of *The Ring and the Book.*

" But I think I gave you as good !
   ' That foreign fellow—who can know
  ' How she pays, in a playful mood,
   ' For his tuning her that piano ? '

" Could you say so, and never say
   ' Suppose we join hands and fortunes,
  ' And I fetch her from over the way,
   ' Her, piano, and long tunes and short tunes ? ' "

Browning's emotion in turning the leaves of the Book he found in Florence, the reader of *Master Hugues of Saxe-Gotha* might suppose him to feel in turning the leaves of an English Dictionary.

" A spirit laughs and leaps through every limb,
  And lights my eye, and lifts me by the hair,
  Letting me have my will again with these." [1]

Strength, sweetness, discord and melody are jostled together in his pages ; but even amid the distracting metaphysics of his later volumes, we are constantly arrested by strains which prove that the philosopher has not absorbed the poet.

---

[1] *The Ring and the Book,* I., 776-778.

The harshness of much of Browning's verse is undeniable. The author himself admits it. Yet he holds, as his defence, that harshness also has its uses.

" ' Touch him ne'er so lightly, into song he broke :
Soil so quick receptive,—not one feather-seed,
Not one flower-dust fell but straight its fall awoke
Vitalizing virtue : song would song succeed
Sudden and spontaneous—prove a poet-soul ! '
                                        Indeed ?
Rock's the song-soil rather, surface hard and bare :
Sun and dew their mildness, storm and frost their
    rage
Vainly both expend,—few flowers awaken there :
Quiet in its cleft broods—what the after age
Knows and names a pine, a nation's heritage."

Each class of poetic as of natural creation has its own laws. The drama, of necessity, cannot have the lyric's "linked sweetness"; and Browning's dramatic pieces demand, by reason of their subject and treatment, a soil even more rocky than that of the ordinary drama. His choice of subject is the root of his "perverse harshness." The question is, whether the discussion of religious and artistic metaphysics, or the making of a lawyer's Latin speech, is a soil possible for poetic growth. The products which have forced their way to light amid these rocks, we must leave to an "after age" to "know and name."

Boldness has been the poet's advocate from first to last. He has entered the first doors of Busyrane, although he has sometimes forgotten the inscription on the last door. [1] "Sense above sound" has been his timely motto for the present day. [2] Yet Beauty is the only elixir of

---

[1] " And, as she lookt about, she did behold
　　How over that same dore was likewise writ,
　　Be bolde, be bolde, and every where, *Be bold;*
　　That much she muz'd, yet could not construe it
　　By any ridling skill, or commune wit.
　　At last she spyde at that rowmes upper end
　　Another yron dore, on which was writ,
　　Be not too bold; whereto though she did bend
　　Her earnest minde, yet wist not what it might
　　　　intend."
　　　　—*The Faerie Queene,* book iii., canto xi., 54.

[2] " The admiration of ancient authors, the hate of the schoolmen, the exact study of languages, . . .

of Wisdom. In Browning's latest works, as in those of Wordsworth, of Carlyle, and even of Goethe, we see the tendency of artists past their maturity to grow impatient of restrictions, to prefer didactic themes, and more and more to neglect, both in conception and in style, the vital principles of artistic creation.

Browning's "obscurity" is almost inseparable from his "harshness." In the one case as in the other, we must understand before we censure. The difficulty of any great thinker's poetry is constantly magnified by those who have seen little of it. *Sordello, Fifine at the Fair, Prince*

---

did bring in an affectionate study of eloquence and copie of speech. . . . This grew speedily to an excess ; for men began to hunt more after words than matter ; more after the choiceness of the phrase, and the round and clean composition of the sentence, and the sweet falling of the clauses, and the varying and illustration of their works with tropes and figures, than after the weight of matter, worth of subject, soundness of argument, life of invention, or depth of jndgement."—*Of the Advancement of Learning.* Book I.

Hohenstiel-Schwangau, and *Red Cotton Night-Cap Country,* one or two of our author's lyrics and romances, as *Childe Roland,* and many of his latest metaphysical and critical pieces are certainly hard reading. With a few exceptions, none of his poems can be called simple. But their author " never pretended to offer such literature as should be a substitute for a cigar or a game at dominoes to an idle man."[1] There is a passage in Carlyle's Essay on Goethe's *Helena* which is so appropriate a defence of the so-called " obscurity " of Browning's best poems, as to justify my adaptation of some sentences :—

" If an artist has conceived his subject in the secret shrine of his own mind, and knows, with a knowledge beyond all power of cavil, that it is true and pure, he may choose his own manner of exhibiting it, and will generally be the fittest to choose it well. One degree of

---

[1] From one of Browning's letters.

light, he may find, will beseem one delineation ; quite a different degree of light another. The face of Agamemnon was not painted but hidden in the old picture : the Veiled Figure at Sais was the most expressive in the Temple. . . . Under Goethe's management, this style of composition has often a singular charm. The reader is kept on the alert, ever conscious of his own active co-operation: light breaks on him, and clearer and clearer vision, by degrees ; till at last the whole lovely Shape comes forth, definite, it may be, and bright with heavenly radiance, or fading, on this side and that, into vague expressive mystery, but true in both cases, and beautiful with nameless enchantments, as the poet's own eye may have beheld it. We love it the more for the labour it has given us : we almost feel as if we ourselves had assisted in its creation. . . . A reposing state, in which the Hill of Vision were brought under us, not we obliged to mount it, might indeed for the present be more convenient ; but, in the end, it could not be equally satisfying. Continuance of passive pleasure, it should never be forgotten, is here, as under all conditions of mortal existence, an impossibility. . . . It is not what we *receive*, but what we are made to *give*, that chiefly contents and profits us. True, the mass of readers will object ; because, like the mass of men, they are too indolent. But if any one affect, not the active and watchful, but the passive and somnolent line of study, are there not writers expressly fashioned for him, enough and to spare ? It is but the smaller number of books that become more instructive by a second perusal : the great majority are as perfectly plain as perfect triteness can make them."

The difficulties which meet the student of Browning's poetry are, not only over-stated but often mis-stated. It is instructive to trace them to their sources.

In Browning's style there is less verbal

or grammatical difficulty than is commonly supposed. A few mannerisms such as "i' the," and "o' the," an occasional involved or clumsy sentence, more often the persistent tracking of some conceit, or a pedantic and obscure allusion, are the main superficial perplexities in his poems. Steeped in Greek, Rabbinical and Mediæval history and art, the most learned of our living poets, he refuses to realise that the majority of his readers are ignorant.

But the essential "obscurity" of the poet's style is inherent in the originality of his conceptions. His subjects are often not only profound, but rare ; they demand from the student an exercise not only of his metaphysical, but of his practically analytic powers. Accuracy and precision are, as a rule, more fairly rated than sympathy of thought. Though *In Memoriam* is in many respects a more difficult poem than *The Ring and the Book*, it appeals to faculties usually better

trained.   For one reader who can
track in a drama the undercurrents of
an individual mood, a hundred will
be found who can enjoy a poem of
reflective sentiment.   The difficulty is
thus primarily one of subject and conception.   In the microscopic subtlety necessary to Browning's purpose, terseness and
diffuseness are alike unavoidable ; but
neither commissions nor omissions are
so much of words as of thoughts.   If
by "obscurity" is meant a looseness of
grasp or haziness of expression, Browning is guiltless.   "He is something too
much the reverse of obscure ; he is too
brilliant and subtle for the ready reader of
a ready writer to follow with any certainty
the track of an intelligence which moves
with such incessant rapidity, or even to
realise with what spider-like swiftness
and sagacity his building spirit leaps and
lightens to and fro and backward and
forward, as it lives along the animated
line of its labour, springs from thread to
thread, and darts from centre to circum-

ference of the glittering and quivering web of living thought, woven from the inexhaustible stores of his perception, and kindled from the inexhaustible fire of his imagination." [1]

This spiderlike method in his dramatic pieces is the essential difficulty in reading Browning. His *Lyrics, Romances, Men and Women,* and *Dramatis Personæ* are, as it were, cocoons, which can only be unravelled, as they were spun, from within.

In his own age it is impossible to determine the place of an original poet ; for the very fact of his originality places him, if not beyond, at least outside of comparison. Yet to reach a true estimate of his originality it is serviceable to contrast him with his predecessors. Much has been written to indicate and illustrate the distinction between Shakespeare's and Browning's art. The difference, apart from

---

[1] *George Chapman: a Critical Essay,* by A. C. Swinburne.

the question as to their relative greatness, is characteristic of the difference between their times. The common statement that Shakespeare reveals his characters acting, while Browning reveals them thinking, suggests, but does not define, the contrast ; for the contrast is not only one of method, but of subject and purpose. To the author of *Hamlet* the drama was the creation of a world of deed and speech, of character as it expressed itself through the action and interaction of circumstance. Even in that play in which the thought and treatment are most akin to those of modern times, the inner world is never bared before us: the dramatist refuses to analyse. The currents of the soul, if they must be shown, are physically re-presented, as in the appearance of the Ghost. We catch the tone of irony in Hamlet's conversations with the King, Polonius, and the courtiers ; we note his conflicting shame and pity for his mother ; we observe his confidence in his friend, and justify his distrust of his love. But the current of outward action moves on ; save for a half-conscious re-velation in soliloquy, the unseen world of thought remains, as in life, "an open secret." A half-conscious revelation of a mood in soliloquy. " The rest is silence," which the dramatist has left for the analysts of after times to break.

Browning is creator and analyst in one. Even in his " dramas," the ordinary method of presentation is reversed. The evolution of incident is sacrificed to the re-velation of character ; and he is ever leav-ing and interrupting the progress of the action for the minute display of shifting moods and motives. Art is a compromise ; and in making this choice, the artist had to make sacrifices. This concentra-tion of focus led him, as we have seen, to a smaller canvas in his dramatic " studies." Under the microscope sec-tions alone can be seen. What has been gained in intensity, has been lost in ex-tension.

It is needless to demand from this modern dramatic method, the archi-tectonic power of Shakspeare's conception which, in the very moment of creation, selects and moulds the diverse scenes and characters into a unity, in which each reflects and supplies what is wanting in the rest. To Browning a monologue, or at most a dialogue, is adequate. A moment or an incident is all that can be brought within his focus. The form of presentation may be varied by dramatic narrative. The studies may even, as in *The Ring and the Book*, be ranged together as a series. But every work of Browning's derives its essential unity (or series of unities) from the creation of a character or a mood. Shakspeare's men and women are a world ; Browning's world is a collection of *Men and Women*.

Yet the sacrifice of synthetic unity is balanced by qualities which are to us eminently serviceable. This new dramatic method is especially fitted for the "minute display," not only of subtle currents of emotion and of modern apparitions of character, but of the infinite complexities of life and thought which this fresh consciousness has brought along with it. In his works the horizon of history has been illumined, and by the interpretation of a past age he has interpreted his own. From the problems of psychology he has turned to those of justice and expediency, of religion and art, and in each he has sought the solution, not by abstract analysis of principles, but by the dramatic creation of individual instances.

The poet's defence of this application of his art is to be found throughout his works. We choose the short poem which opens his volume *Men and Women* as the most succinct and explicit. *Transcendentalism* may be called Browning's *Apologia pro Arte Suâ*. The author interrupts the supposed writer of a poem in Twelve Books entitled "Transcendentalism."

" Stop playing, poet !　May a brother speak ?
　'Tis you speak, that's your error.　Song's our art :
　Whereas you please to speak these naked thoughts
　Instead of draping them in sights and sounds.
　—True thoughts, good thoughts, thoughts fit to
　　　treasure up !
　But why such long prolusion and display,
　Such tuning and adjustment of the harp,
　And taking it upon your breast, at length,
　Only to speak dry words across its strings ?
　Stark-naked thought is in request enough :
　Speak prose, and hollo it till Europe hears !　.　.　.

　　" But here's your fault ; grown men want thought,
　　　you think ;
　　Thought's what they mean by verse, and seek in
　　　verse ?
　　Boys seek for images and melody,
　　Men must have reason— so, you aim at men.
　　Quite otherwise !　Objects throng our youth, 'tis
　　　true ;
　　We see and hear and do not wonder much :
　　If you could tell us what they mean, indeed ! "

This, concludes Browning, is the
end of art.　Take the musty Boehme
and his thought-lore.　What has his
volume of mystical abstraction regarding
plants done for us?

" We shut the clasps and find life's summer past.
  Then, who helps more, pray, to repair our loss ? "

Is it not the poet, the " makar,"

> " Who made things Boehme wrote thoughts
>   about ?   .
> He with a 'look you ! ' vents a brace of rhymes,
> And in there breaks the sudden rose herself,
> Over us, under, round us every side,
> Nay, in and out the tables and the chairs
> And musty volumes, Boehme's book and all—
> Buries us with a glory, young once more,
> Pouring heaven into this shut house of life.

" So come, the harp back to your heart again !
  You are a poem, though your poem's naught ! " . .

We have here the *raison d'être*, not only
of the poet but of the dramatist, as
the interpreter. Not in criticisms or
theories, but in creations, are the
thoughts of our age to be re-
presented. To realise life to any purpose, we must see it in living men and
women. Their thoughts and passions
must become " incidents in the development of a human soul."

This poem is not the defence only of the dramatist's analytic, but of his "realistic" method. The realism of our present art has taken many phases: all can be ranged under two classes. There is the realism which pictures for us the the most trivial or the most repulsive details of life, with no object save to satisfy the craving of unimaginative minds for the sensation of stupidity or of horror, for no reason except that they are more or less accurate photographs of what exists. This realism through which we see no imaginative light or spiritual meaning, we do not find in Browning's work. There is much minute detail of what in life seems insignificant or unpleasant. But his purpose is to "tell us what they mean," to "pour heaven into this shut house of life. Pippa passing through the streets of Asolo—in itself a "small event"—sings and proves, "there is no last nor first." The passion of Ottima and the villainy of Guido are ugly facts;

but the wreck they work is not final. Their setting is not a melodrama, but a tragedy.

Browning is the optimist of our age ; and his optimism is that of a fearless imagination. The dramatist has not hesitated to strike the discords of the individual life, but he has resolved them into fresh harmonies :

> " The high that proved too high, the heroic for earth too hard,
>> The passion that left the ground to lose itself in the sky,
>> Are music sent up to God by the lover and the bard." [1]

Tennyson soothes with a melody of doubt and hope : Browning inspires with a strong and living faith. Tennyson enlarges our horizon : Browning braces us with mountain air. The one strains his eyes for the infinite vision : the other exults in man's present imperfection, and sees " the Christ that is to be," " a god though in the germ."

---

[1] *Abt Vogler.*

" ' Tis a clay cast, the perfect thing." [1]

Andrea del Sarto, called " the faultless painter," failed and recognised his failure.

" Not on the vulgar mass
       Called ' work,' must sentence pass,
Things done, that took the eye and had the price ;
       O'er which, from level stand,
       The low world laid its hand,
Found straightway to its mind, could value in a trice.

" But all, the world's coarse thumb
       And finger failed to plumb,
So passed in making up the main account ;
       All instincts immature,
       All purposes unsure,
That weighed not as his work, yet swelled the man's
       amount.

" Thoughts hardly to be packed
       Into a narrow act,
Fancies that broke through language and escaped ;
       All I could never be,
       All, men ignored in me,
This, I was worth to God, whose wheel the pitcher
       shaped." [2]

---

[1] *James Lee's Wife.*
[2] *Rabbi ben Ezra.*

Life's success is not in attainment but in endeavour.

" It is but to keep the nerves at strain,
    To dry one's eyes and laugh at a fall,
And, baffled, get up and begin again,—
    So the chace takes up one's life, that's all . . .
No sooner the old hope goes to ground
    Than a new one, straight to the self-same mark,
I shape me—
Ever
Removed ! " [1]

The unpardonable sin in this eternal imperfection and eternal progress is to think we have attained the goal.

" Nothing can be as it hath been before ;
    Better, so call it, only not the same.
To draw one beauty into our hearts' core,
    And keep it changeless ! such our claim ;
So answered,—Never more !

" Simple?   Why this is the old woe o' the world,
    Tune, to whose rise and fall we live and die.
Rise with it, then !   Rejoice that man is hurled
    From change to change unceasingly,
His soul's wings never furled." [2]

---

[1] *Life in a Love.*
[2] *James Lee's Wife.*

This is the dominant note of Browning's
work ; the key to his interpretation of
the world's "apparent failures ;" the
central principle by which he reads and
re-creates in his gallery the story of
life, religion, and art. These three are
one in his poetry. "Out of the three
sounds he frames not a fourth sound,
but a star." Devotee and artist both see

> "On the earth the broken arcs ; in the heaven, a
>   perfect round."

But while the one turns his eyes beyond,
the imagination of the other rejoices in
earth's joys and promises :

> " For pleasant is this flesh ;
>   Our soul, in its rose mesh
> Pulled ever to the earth, still yearns for rest ;
>   Would we some prize might hold
>   To match those manifold
> Possessions of the brute,—gain most, as we did best !
>
>   Let us not always say,
>   ' Spite of this flesh to-day
> ' I strove, made head, gained ground upon the
>   whole !'

> As the bird wings and sings
>   Let us cry ' All good things
> ' Are ours, nor soul helps flesh more, now, than flesh
>   helps soul ! ' "[1]

Evil, suffering, and sorrow have their uses.   Norbert counts

> " Life just a stuff
> To try the soul's strength on, to educe the man."

Sebald is "proud to feel such torments;" Pompilia's woes have wrought a sweetness in her soul.

> " Then, welcome each rebuff
>   That turns earth's smoothness rough,
> Each sting that bids nor sit nor stand but go !
>   Be our joys three parts pain !
>   Strive, and hold cheap the strain ;
> Learn, nor account the pang ; dare, never grudge the
>   throe ! . . .

> What is he but a brute
>   Whose flesh has soul to suit,
> Whose spirit works lest arms and legs want play ?
>   To man, propose this test—
>   Thy body at its best,
> How far can that project thy soul on its lone way ?

---

[1] *Rabbi Ben Ezra.*

Yet gifts should prove their use :
I own the Past profuse
Of power each side, perfection every turn :
Eyes, ears took in their dole,
Brain treasured up the whole ;
Should not the heart beat once, ' How good to live
and learn ? '

Not once beat ' Praise be Thine !
' I see the whole design,
' I, who saw power, see new love perfect too :
' Perfect I call Thy plan :
' Thanks that I was a man !
' Maker, remake, complete,—I trust what Thou shalt
do ! ' ' "

www.ingramcontent.com/pod-product-compliance
Lightning Source LLC
Chambersburg PA
CBHW030604040726
47497CB00008B/2837